THE NEW GOD

JEFFREY THOMAS

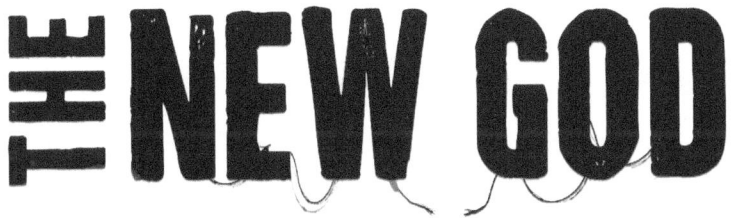

THE NEW GOD

A Punktown Novel

WEIRD HOUSE

ISBN: 978-1-957121-86-4

Text © 2024 by Jeffrey Thomas

Cover Artwork © 2024 by Michael Squid

Interior and cover design by César Puch

Editor and Publisher, Joe Morey

Weird House Press
Central Point, OR 97502
www.weirdhousepress.com

Praise for Jeffrey Thomas' Punktown series

"Fans of cyberpunk noir and Lovecraftian horror will find much to enjoy."
—*Publishers Weekly*

"Punktown is searing and alien and anxious and rich, and it is humane, and it is moving."
—*China Mieville*

"Punktown is on the verge of becoming one of those classic, timeless destinations for dark fantasy and SF readers."
—*Jeff VanderMeer*

"A dazzlingly complex and detailed future vision as poetic as it is horrifying, full of insights and images that cling to the mind."
—*Ramsey Campbell*

"Terrifically vital, violent, and imaginative."
—*Ellen Datlow*

"Punktown has the chaotic immediacy and lived-in feel of a real place."
—*The Guardian*

"All the gritty immediacy and romantic cynicism of classic cyberpunk, along with morally complex, vividly disturbing evocations of supernatural eruptions and corruptions."
—*Locus*

For author and editor Brian M. Sammons, whose game scenario *Looking Long Into the Abyss*, from the manual *Punktown: A Setting Book for Call of Cthulhu® and Basic Roleplaying* (Miskatonic River Press/Chronicle City/Chaosium Inc., 2017), formed the basis for this story.

"Those who fight monsters should take care that they never become one."
—Friedrich Nietzsche

Prologue
Night on the Town

Tam Vonner wandered from room to room of his thirtieth-floor apartment, sipping from a steamy mug of the mustard drink his people favored, thinking about tonight's planned get-together with his old friend, Colin Rex.

Being situated toward the center of the apartment tower, Tam's flat had no windows, but a floor-to-ceiling virtual screen automatically followed him as he paced, sliding along the walls, giving him a view of a city that sprawled to every horizon. Officially, this megalopolis was named Paxton, but of course it was only officials who called it that. To everyone else, it was Punktown.

Even as high up as his flat was, plenty of other towers out there were so tall he couldn't see their tops from here. Punktown was packed solid with buildings, and gave the impression of being multiple cities superimposed over each other. There was the city of gargantuan, god-like skyscrapers, and if someone told you they pierced the mesosphere you might believe them. Buttressing these titans was a city of lesser, but still lofty, structures. And then there were the most abundant buildings, squatting closer to the streets, whether these were housed apartments or places of business or both. The city's multitudinous buildings had been constructed in a wide variety of styles, from a wide variety of materials, by a wide variety of sentient races. The only characteristic they all shared was *light*. As night descended on Punktown, a dense web of light wove the city together into

1

something almost whole. Glowing windows, colorful neons, dazzling lasers, holograms both stationary and animated. And then there were the roving firefly lights of helicars, in the upper regions, and crisscrossing river currents at street level or along elevated highways. Punktown was like a terrestrial scaffolding supporting artificial constellations. It was a persuasive mirage. The metropolis seemed to want to trick its inhabitants into believing it was greater than the actual cosmos beyond, which it blotted out with all its color, magnitude, and distracting clamor.

Though this was the only world Tam had ever known, strangely tonight the view inspired vertigo, and the galaxies of lights were giving him a headache. But the truth was, he hadn't been feeling well today. Maybe it was a barometric pressure headache, he thought. All day, the air outside had been almost solid with humidity, the sky greenish-black with a thunderstorm that had never come, despite intermittent sprinkles of fat hot drops like bullets. The tension in the air remained tangible, like a ceiling of stone that threatened to collapse the towers that upheld it, even though the summer temperature had dropped somewhat with the coming of evening.

With his sinuses feeling packed solid and a vein pulsing along the bridge of his nose, Tam turned toward the viewscreen that had been shadowing him like a loyal dog and commanded, "Stationary." Then: "Mirror." He stepped closer to the screen, and examined his own image. "Magnify face times four," he said.

Tam Vonner was a Choom, one of the indigenous people of this planet—which Earth colonists had generations ago renamed Oasis—and his race was one of the handful that most resembled the Earthers. The only salient difference was the extensive Choom mouth, slicing the cheeks back all the way to the hinges of the jaws. In service of his massive lower jaw, Tam's neck was a solid column of muscles and tendons, though his body's overall frame was slight.

Tam used a lotion to suppress the growth of hair on his head, his bare dome tattooed with a grid of copper traces like a circuit board, a rimmed

2

hole at each nexus point. Many of these small "lands" were active ports serving a variety of purposes, physical connections to the ultranet being foremost, while other lands were merely cosmetic for a uniform effect.

He tilted his head this way and that, examining himself in the reflective screen. Besides his flesh appearing pale and clammy, his eyes looked sunken to him, his cheeks smudgy with gauntness. Not only could he feel a muscle jumping under one eye, he could actually see it twitching in his doppelganger self.

But there was more. "What the blast?" he hissed, reaching up to touch one of the ports in his skull. His fingers came away wet with thick slime, so shiny it was almost silver, and slippery like a lubricant. He smelled the fluid, fearing it was pus, but it had no odor of infection. He used a washcloth to dab at the little orifice until it came away dry, then he poured some disinfectant on a wad of toilet paper and wiped around the area. He's taken some antibiotics, just in case. Rejection of cybernetic enhancements was not uncommon, but he'd had these ports for years and didn't know why one would start troubling him now, unless he had recently plugged in a contaminated jack somewhere.

He considered calling Colin and telling him their excursion tonight might not be a good idea, after all, but it had been difficult getting his boyhood friend to agree to meet up. If he cancelled, who could say when he might coax Colin out again?

A crystalline tone chimed behind him, immediately followed by a familiar feminine voice calling out. "Tam? May I come?"

Even before he started swiveling toward the voice, Tam said, "Missra! Yes ... come."

He completed turning, and she stepped into the room before him. Missra Sang.

Missra's hair was short and dark, her long-lashed eyes oversized like a doll's, at once both dark and clear as amber bottle glass. A cinnamon dusting of freckles across her nose and pale cheekbones, full lips pink as the inside of a conch. She wore a tight and high-collared black t-shirt, and black leggings that clung to voluptuous hips. It might not be noticed immediately that both garments were covered in tiny glimmering dots like immensely distant stars, as if their material had been cut from the fabric of night. She was barefoot. Her looks were all sweet innocence *yin* to unpretentious sexiness *yang*.

"Have you learned anything at all?" she asked, her child-like face pinched and anxious. "Devon still won't even acknowledge me. I need to know what he's up to."

"He's been just as elusive with me as he's been with you, Missra," Tam reported. "I can't get him to talk to me, either."

"Have you tried hacking into his system?"

"Of course I've been trying, but you know Devon. If I'm a tech artist, he's a tech god. He's built a VR library in the ultranet. I've been able to get inside very briefly and copy a little of what I found, but I always get shoved out again—fast. His shields are mutable. Just when you get past them, they morph again ... slip between you and the inside. It's continuous. It's like digging a hole in beach sand in-between breakers."

"Do you think he knows you were in?"

"No, or I'm sure he'd confront me about it."

"So what did you learn?"

"I'll show you, but not tonight. I'm going out shortly to meet a mutual friend of ours."

"Who is that?"

Tam waited a few ticks to draw out the suspense. He was sure she knew the answer. "The equally elusive Colin."

Did he see her jaw tighten a little? Missra said, "Are you sure he'll really be there this time?"

"It sounds like he means it. That's why I can't talk much tonight. I don't want to run the risk of being late, and him vanishing back into Colin-land."

"He still doesn't know? About ... me?"

"I haven't told him."

"You mustn't."

"I won't," Tam promised her. "But someday—"

"I will," Missra assured him.

Tam snapped his head to the left. "Who else is there?" he blurted.

"Tam?" Missra said.

"Did you bring someone else with you?" His eyes darted.

"No, of course not."

He shuffled in a circle, studying every corner of the room, until he faced Missra again. "Sorry ... must've been someone talking in the next apartment."

"Your apartment is soundproofed," Missra reminded him.

"Then maybe it's my subconscious," Tam joked shakily, coming back to himself, "reminding me I should get going to the club."

"I'll catch you at an earlier time tomorrow, to talk about what you've found."

"Not too early," he said, grinning. "I've scheduled a hangover."

"I'm debating whether to tell you to say hello to Colin for me. Maybe you shouldn't mention me. I don't want to hurt him."

"Too late for that, beautiful," Tam told her.

"More than I already have," Missra amended. Then she turned away, to pad from the room on her bare feet. Over her shoulder she called back to her friend, "Have fun." Then she was gone.

One
Unreality Affliction

The patrons of Club Feel were literally bouncing off the walls, leaping into the air and crashing into each other, tossing themselves to the floor and rolling to their feet again, glassy-eyed and grinning. As Colin Rex entered Feel and glanced toward the dance floor, he saw one young woman whipping her sweaty tresses across the faces of others who danced close to her, all the while laughing deliriously, despite having blood from a broken nose smeared across her cheeks. No matter; Daddy would have her all patched up and respectable looking by tomorrow afternoon.

Feel was an upscale nightclub and disco off Beaumonde Square, the city's most affluent sector. To aid in giving the clientele more bounce, the dance floor was cushioned with one continuous sheet of bioengineered human flesh. The establishment's walls were of various other materials and textures. Colin saw one man, having stripped his shirt off, rubbing his back up and down violently against a wall as rough as 40-grit sandpaper, scraping his skin raw. A Choom woman hugged a support column that was covered in fur, her eyes closed in bliss.

Two security guards rushed the dance floor to seize a young man who had seemingly fallen onto his face, hoisting him to his feet. Through the crowd, Colin saw that the man had actually opened a wound in the organic floor with a knife, and had been copulating with it. Blood smudged his belly, and he laughed with joy as the security men strong-armed him. Colin was sure the man invited the pain.

"Hey, gorgeous," a Tikkihotto male purred to Colin, the humanoid leaning in close in an attempt to caress Colin's face with the translucent optical tendrils that sprouted from his skull sockets. Colin caught the man by the throat and held him away at arm's length. The reaching organs contracted and trembled. "I just wanted to feel you," the Tikkihotto choked.

"It will be the last thing you feel if you try it again," Colin said in his typical low-key murmur. He shoved the Tikkihotto away in dismissal, continued making his way through the packed room in search of the friend he had come to meet.

Colin Rex was athletic in build but not muscle-bound, and overall perhaps too good-looking for his own taste. Many people in his line of work had grown up on the streets, had belonged to raggedy brawling gangs. Not him. His parents had been well-off, and so they'd been able to custom design their son, right down to ensuring that he *was* a son. So his short, neatly-cut hair was blond, his eyes blue, his jaw firm, his features almost blandly perfect. He often self-consciously counteracted the effect, somewhat, by often going unshaven for days, like now. He was not so rueful about his looks, though, to have hesitated in having the ruined portion of his face made whole again, when he'd once lost an eye to an enemy's beam weapon. He'd even paid to have his eye cloned back *in situ*, rather than make do with a synthetic one. He'd never told his parents, so as not to upset them, and they'd never been aware of this injury.

The black suit he wore tonight was custom-fitted and expensive, but once again in crude contrast, like his scruffy beard, under his unbuttoned jacket he wore a sleeveless white t-shirt. The lining of his jacket was a tight mesh that could shield the wearer from various types of ray beams, and keep solid bullets from penetrating flesh, though they might still inflict blunt trauma. In a shoulder holster under his jacket he carried a handgun. That was hardly unusual, however, in this city—which was infamous for its population of criminals. Of whom Colin Rex was just one.

Colin was thirty-two. Ten years ago, he'd have been carrying four guns on his person, and a boot knife. But over time he'd come to find these accoutrements too bulky, distracting … so he'd pared it down to one. It felt lighter, freer. If you were facing one enemy, one gun was enough. If you were facing multiple enemies, it was always possible to adopt their own weapons against them. The most enemies he'd ever killed in one fight—an ambush by an up-and-coming competitor, and the battle that had temporarily cost him an eye—was five. He'd killed the first two men with his own gun, the last three with theirs.

He was a little faster, a little stronger, and even without expensive medical procedures healed a little better than natural-borns. His parents had made certain their only child was well-designed in all regards, though he knew he had gravely disappointed them with the manner in which he had applied his gifts, the direction he had taken in life. In premature retirement, a few years ago they had moved to that other titanic colony-city, Miniosis, to be away from Punktown. Perhaps, too, to be away from him.

Having thoroughly checked out the club, he determined his friend Tam Vonner hadn't arrived yet, so he took a table to wait for him. A fragment of Colin's mind wondered if some enemy had paid Tam to lure him here in another ambush, but he knew Tam better than that. It was simply reflexive paranoia, part of the skill set that kept him alive.

With a satisfying *clack* he flipped a switch to call up the drink selection from the menu screen that formed the table's surface. The food and drink menu was orange text against a black background, and to advance the text Colin had to turn a dial that clicked in increments. The beige-colored frame that bordered the glossy menu screen was pebbly in texture, while the knobs and buttons of the screen controls were translucent and lit up orange when activated. All this tactility was deliberate, taking the place of intangible holographic screens and control panels that might be conjured and manipulated with hand movements, verbal directions, or even by thought commands. This retro approach had been the style throughout the Earth Colonies for the past few years, in response to a condition that many sociologists warned was affecting more and more people—this being a sense of disconnection or displacement from the physical world. An overreliance on virtual as opposed to physical activities, an overabundance of time spent working and playing in the ultranet, had resulted in increasing numbers of people feeling "unreal." Establishments like Feel were another response to that same societal condition.

Tam had discussed UA—this so-called Unreality Affliction—with Colin in the past. "Ah, it's just a rich people's sickness," Tam had scoffed. "It's another fad illness to feed their self-absorption."

"Couldn't their self-absorption be a symptom of the affliction?" Colin had countered, playing devil's advocate. He'd hoped he didn't sound like he was being defensive about his parents.

"Their self-absorption isn't a symptom of being removed from corporeality—it's a symptom of being removed from the real world. That's not the same thing. They're too wealthy to suffer like the common folk do, so they have to invent their own brand-named suffering. Hey, you know me. I spend half my life in the ultranet, and I don't feel any less real for it."

That was true enough. Colin didn't know anyone more technologically oriented than Tam Vonner. Tam was a first-rate hacker, a cyber-scrounger, and expert in all things tech. But where Colin belonged to a syndy—the Jolly Bill Family—Tam was a freelancer, selling his skills to anyone with enough munits. Both men were versatile in their own ways. As friends in their youth they had started out much the same, sharing a fairly privileged upbringing, but Colin had gone down a more shadowed road, and Tam had numerous times tried to call him back from it. But Colin just didn't have Tam's skills, nor his parents' financial acumen; he'd had to develop cruder talents. In his virtual realm, Tam never had to handle illegal drugs, steal physical materials, break bones. Kill. Tam had offered to teach his friend tech skills ... even get Colin chip-implanted and upload knowledge straight to his brain if he had to, because technically speaking anyone was capable of learning anything in such a manner. Though, just as there was little need for people to endure disability or deformity in these times, whether or not the average person could *afford* implanted knowledge or physical health was another matter. Munits ruled all, and the people with the most munits tended to want to hoard them. How else could the proper social structures be maintained? That is, how else could one enjoy the fruits of privilege unless by contrast with the fruitless?

In any event, though money wasn't the issue in his own case, Colin had declined his friend's offers. He was already by then well on his path, committed to those he had sworn allegiance to. Or to sum it up to Tam, with the barest smile Colin had said, "Already damned."

Before Colin could punch his order into the table, an attentive waitress came over to take it in person. She was striking, a blue-skinned Sinanese—another of the most human of all sentient races—but she was twitching involuntarily. First a shoulder, then her head on its slim neck, then half her face, as if a centipede of electricity were scurrying about madly throughout her body. Colin ordered a whiskey.

"Don't you want something *spicier*?" the waitress asked. She obviously practiced what she preached. She gestured toward a nearby table, where a young couple were taking turns squirting atomized mist down their throats from a small metal orb. "To get your adrenaline flowing, your nerves humming, so you'll *feel*?"

"I just want to feel mellow," Colin said in his laconic mumble, smiling at her faintly, which was the most he ever smiled.

Charmed by what she took for shyness, the waitress stroked his face before turning away to fill his order. She was too lovely for Colin to want to seize by the throat, though he was put off by the way she wobbled precariously on her spike heels as she twitched away. She looked buffeted by the pulse of booming music, that bounced against Colin's eardrums like the crashing dancers on the skin floor.

His whiskey came only partly spilled by his spasmodic waitress, and he was just taking his first sip when a familiar voice observed, "Couldn't wait for me, huh? Or do you need a drink before you see my ugly face?"

Colin swiveled a little in his seat, took Tam Vonner's hand and pulled himself to his feet to fold his friend in a brief embrace. Then he held the Choom away and said, "Uglier than ever."

"The years aren't kind to any of us. And it has been over a year since I've seen you, you know. I might start thinking you're dodging me."

Colin smiled. "It's an awful big town. Too much space between people."

"Whatever you say." They both sat down.

"Seriously ... you don't look good." Colin leaned forward over the menu screen, his expression concerned. "You're sweating like you came out of a sauna. You okay?"

Tam wiped the sweat from his eyes with the palms of his hands. "Yeah ... just not enough sleep, I guess."

"There're pills for that."

"To sleep better, or stay awake better?"

"Whatever works."

"Ah, it's this latest job I've been running. I'm just wiped ... no worries." Tam stretched his huge Choom's grin so wide it seemed it might travel to the back of his skull and take the whole top of his head off. "Hey, we're here to have fun tonight, right? Like the old days. Drink, drugs, dance, dames."

"Dames," Colin echoed. "Where'd you get that?"

"Old Earth movies."

"I'll pass on the drugs."

"Just sell 'em, don't do 'em anymore, huh?"

Colin stared at Tam for a long silent moment, then raised his glass for a sip. In a cooler tone he said, "I'll pass on the dames, too."

"Oh, you're no fun in your old age, man. Can you at least help *me* find a dame? We can trick her into thinking you're taking her home, but she'll wake up tomorrow with me in her bed."

"Sounds like a plan," Colin said, wary of his friend's next dig.

The Sinanese waitress returned, and Tam ordered a metal orb of a legal stimulant called Jet; the same that the couple at the next table had been squirting down their throats. They had since left their seats to thrash against each other and strangers on the dance floor.

"How are things on the gangland front?" Tam asked Colin after he had shot a few jets against the back of his throat.

"Now I know why I dodge you," Colin said. He made it sound like it was only a joke.

"Seriously, I'm always afraid the Teeb Family is going to get sick of you upstart Jolly Bill folks and grind you all under their heel."

"Neptune Teeb's getting old. And he recognizes this is a big city. Jolly Bill's no upstart—he's been running his operation for going on twenty years."

"But he was always small fish. Past few years he's gotten bigger. With the help of dedicated workers like you."

"Can we talk about something else?"

"Such as?"

"Have you seen Missra lately?"

Tam sprayed some more Jet. "Missra," he repeated, bobbing his head. "I'm surprised you even ask. You haven't tried to seek her out yourself, to see how she's been doing? Oh, that's right … it's a big town. Too much space between people."

"I asked you a simple question."

"I see her. I saw her tonight, in fact."

"Really?" Colin said. "And?"

"And what?"

"She ever ask about me?"

"What do you think?" Tam seemed to watch Colin's face carefully. "And aren't you going to ask how the Third Musketeer is doing? Devon?"

Colin only said, "And where'd you get that, Third Musketeer? Another old Earth movie?"

"*What?*" Tam suddenly whipped his head to one side, eyes gone wide. "Dung, man, did you hear that voice?"

"Voice? I only hear bad music."

"What the blast was it *saying?*"

"Hey." Colin touched his arm. "You sure you're okay?"

Once more wiping away sweat that had gathered in his eyebrows, Tam faced forward again. "Yeah … sorry, man … must've just been somebody at another table. What'd you say again?"

"Nothing."

The Choom set his orb down abruptly and shot up from his seat, looking right and left. "I want to dance."

"I'll sit this one out, but thanks for asking."

"Not with you, pretty boy. See anything promising?"

"Just go up on the floor and throw yourself into everybody. Something might stick."

Tam leaned in close and shouted over a surge in the music as a new track started up, "I'll do that!" Then he turned away and skipped toward the springy living dance floor, like a swimmer running up to the diving board.

Colin watched him, feeling a mixture of fondness as if for a brother, and regret for coming here tonight. But Tam had been so insistent this time. Colin couldn't dodge him forever.

Tam was bounding around out there with abandon, swinging his arms wildly and accidentally striking others around him, who seemed to welcome the brute sensation. He caught Colin observing him, and flashed a grin. Colin was embarrassed for his friend's lack of reserve, but couldn't help smiling back at him. Tam hopped nearer to a sweat-shiny Black woman who was whipping her hair around like a propeller: long braided ropes studded with glowing beads. He closed his eyes and let her cat o' nine tails slash across his face. Rather than having suddenly accepted the theory of Unreality Affliction, though, Colin felt his friend—never popular with the opposite sex—simply relished female contact of any sort.

Colin took another sip of his whiskey, making it last because he was not in the habit of becoming intoxicated and thus vulnerable in public, sweeping the club with his gaze to be certain no potential enemies had slipped in while he'd been distracted with Tam. Old habits that kept him from dying hard.

When he returned his attention to the dance floor, he was perplexed to find Tam had apparently vanished. Had he been dragged off by that exuberant propeller-haired woman, after he had made himself an eager victim of her lashings? But no, there she was, still flinging herself about as if in some feverish ceremony, worked up to believe she'd been possessed by spirits.

Then Colin saw Tam. He lay on his face on the floor of bioengineered flesh, while others sprang up and down all around him, mostly oblivious. Had he thrown himself down to experience the sensation of bare skin—hopefully not to the extent of that man security had dragged off—or had he tripped? The idea flashed to Colin that maybe Tam himself had been accidentally struck by an elbow, or maybe not-so-accidentally struck by someone who hadn't really appreciated the wild flailing of his arms, after all. When Colin saw that his friend didn't appear inclined or able to rise to his feet, he started up from his chair in doubled concern.

But then Tam *did* rise up—with startling abruptness, like a marionette whose owner had suddenly jerked it by its strings. And it was strings that Colin seemed to be seeing, radiating upward from Tam's bald head. These were not taut puppeteer's strings, however, but thin silver tendrils that wavered and coiled. Colin realized that glistening, writhing feelers had extruded themselves from each of the tiny ports inset into Tam's skull.

Tam was seemingly dancing again, but he really wasn't. This time it was more like violent convulsions that made his arms flutter. His whole frame was electrified, like that of a person suffering a grand mal seizure.

Colin had left his seat by now, and was striding toward the dance floor, pushing men and women and nonhuman beings out of his way without regard. When one man protested and surged back at him, Colin chopped him across the Adam's apple without even really looking at him.

Some of the dancing club patrons were finally noticing something was off with Tam, and moved back to stare at him, but most were still thrashing heedlessly. Through the chaos of their frenetic bodies, Colin couldn't be sure of what he saw next, but it appeared that one of Tam's hands was flung off its wrist by the force of his erratic movements. No, he wasn't misinterpreting: he clearly saw Tam's other hand go sailing up over the

14

heads of the dancers, striking the dance space's back wall. Colin imagined, rather than heard, the splat sound it made.

And in the next instant, Tam's head came off. It rocketed up away from his body like a champagne cork, on its downward arc striking one of the dancers hard on the shoulder. The impact bowled the dancer to the floor, and Colin saw his friend's head roll between people's legs. They jumped back in revulsion to make way for it.

From Tam's open neck jetted mists of arctic cold. These white clouds also gushed from the ends of both his crazily gesticulating arms. Along with these jets, from the nozzles of his wrists and the crater of his neck burst many more of the same silver tendrils that had a moment ago erupted through Tam's i/o ports. These bundles of noodle-like tendrils blew wildly, like ribbons tied to the grille of a fan. The gusting icy air made a terrible whistling howl, not only from Tam's neck but from the ends of his arms as well. Unless that was his new voice.

Tam's left arm swung back across a woman's face, and the blow didn't look accidental. Even over the bass-heavy music that thudded against Colin's eardrums, he thought he heard the crack of bone as the woman dropped.

Colin kept moving through the intervening bodies, and now his hand was slipping under his jacket to grip the handle of his pistol, which was a .55 Revenant.

The thing that had been Tam pivoted toward a male dancer, who had finally glommed that things were not good and was turning away to bolt. Tam's right arm shot out and caught the young man's head in its whipping tendrils. They wrapped around his face, across his eyes and his open, screaming mouth. The man's hair rippled in the concentrated hurricane of frigid air so close beside him.

Some clubs scanned their clientele at the door and confiscated and tagged their weapons. Club Feel did not. As this was Punktown, guns were almost a prerequisite. Even as Colin drew his own handgun, he saw a half dozen others rise up almost in unison. These club patrons assumed a shooter's stance—either precise, or sloppily drunken—and soon the air was crackling with gunfire that kicked against Colin's ears even more loudly than the music.

Solid bullets made of soft mushrooming metal, or hard-jacketed rocketing metal. Projectiles that burrowed through flesh and blew blood on walls never went out of style, any more than did knives and bats. But there were also red streaking ray bolts. One of these beams missed Tam and burned a black hole in the throat of the man whose head was engulfed in squeezing tendrils. He went limp. The tendrils loosened their grip, let him drop. Colin saw the man's face was crusted white with ice crystals.

Tam jumped and juddered with the impacts that pounded across his body like a meteor shower blowing craters in a moon, but he still managed to stay on his feet ... still managed to lunge forward. He swung his left arm again, striking one of the shooters so hard that the man flew back and knocked two other gunmen to the floor. Their pistols strafed the ceiling. The floor, too, was bleeding from a number of bullet wounds.

After shoving one last person out of his way, Colin held the Revenant at arm's length. His ammo was different from what had been fired so far. There were three grades of plasma ammunition available in Punktown. Red plasma ate a small hole. Blue plasma was more voracious, but only consumed organic matter. Green plasma—the most expensive type, the hardest to come by—didn't care what it ate: flesh, concrete, metal. It ate, and it ate. Colin's Revenant was loaded with .55 green plasma gel capsules.

Colin fired three gel bullets straight into his best friend's chest.

With a louder whistling howl from his neck and wrists, Tam immediately seemed determined to rush straight at Colin. Another shooter went flying out of his way, with a broken neck. Colin saw that Tam had snatched a fresh victim with his tendrils, and dragged this man by the throat, his face turning purple and eyes ballooning in their sockets.

Yet the luminous green plasma was spreading across Tam's chest, the three holes widening in mere seconds, the wounds gaping, growing, joining until they became one. And that was when Tam's body separated ... as he was only a few more paces from reaching Colin. Colin stepped back and lowered his handgun to watch.

Within seconds of Tam collapsing at Colin's feet, his torso was gone, eaten away to a smoking sludge that itself ate into the flesh of the floor. But his arms and legs still glowed green at their ends, and the limbs shortened, shortened. The last to go were the tendrils at the wrists, which blackened, shriveled, burned away to ash and to nothingness. A mass of tendrils like a dumped bucketful of worms squirmed on the floor where they had protruded from Tam's neck stump, but they too convulsed in agony as they shortened, and withered, then were gone without a trace.

Cries went up all around. No one at all was dancing, though the music still pulsed as if they were all trapped inside a gigantic heart. Friends or concerned strangers knelt by the dead (Colin counted three) and injured. Someone shouted in his ear, "Man, what the blast *was* that thing?"

He didn't answer this person. His searching eyes found Tam's severed head lying on its cheek on the pillow of flesh floor. He didn't hesitate. He walked toward it, pulling off his suit jacket as he did so. Colin flung his jacket down over the head, over Tam's familiar face—the only portion of him still remaining—and covered it.

Then he crouched down, gathered Tam's head in his jacket, straightened, and ignoring a voice of protest behind him, strode toward the door to leave Club Feel.

Two
From the Ashes

Colin's fellow syndy member Verge lived in an apartment that gazed down into a narrow canyon between two immense housing blocks, the tightly stacked floors of which resembled the pages of a closed, hefty book. Each stratum-like level had a balcony tier which ran the respective building's great length, seemingly unto infinity. Spanning the facing apartment blocks were thick power cables, which daring helicar pilots flew between rather than over or under, and the occasional pedestrian bridge. Here and there, gang banners ragged from the elements and gunfire hung down from the vines of power cables like laundry pinned out to dry.

Colin had parked his hovercar—a hot pink Razur with yellow trim—against the curb far below, and rode up in one of the external freight-type elevators to Verge's ninetieth-level flat. Along the way, a glowing pinkish figure leapt out of nowhere onto the outside of the elevator cage, rattling the mesh and snarling in at him. Colin glared back at the apparition in irritation. It was a hardlight hologram, an advertisement for a movie that had come out almost a decade ago: *Screaming Pink Nazis* (based on the popular breakfast cereal). Through some glitch, throughout the city a number of these holographic entities had persisted long after the movie they had been generated to advertise had flopped and left the theaters.

The elevator jolted to a halt at Verge's balcony. The silently snarling pink ghost scrabbled up and away, out of sight. Colin's coworker, notified in advance, opened his door and waved a mechanical arm that resembled a surgical instrument, inviting him to come inside. Colin did so, carrying a gym bag he had taken from his car's trunk.

"This couldn't wait until morning?" Verge complained.

"You've never heard of decay?" Colin replied.

He had been here before. With all the bejeweled and humming tech crammed into it, Verge's loft-like flat looked more like a research and development lab than an apartment. Colin had to step over power cables that slithered across the floor. Up the walls and across the ceiling, in support cages, were more orderly bundles of cables—color-coded orange, yellow, and blue—all of them thick as a garden hose.

Verge belonged to perhaps the most diminutive race in Punktown— that is, after the termite-like Mee'hi. He resembled an albino newt, four inches from his snout to the tip of his finned tail. To better coexist in a humanoid-oriented society, this tiny being sat in an enclosed cockpit the size of a toaster, supported by three jointed legs, with three artificial arms folded just under the cabin—which had clear windows and yellow flames painted on its sides. Verge's voice came through a speaker, loud and clear and translated into English.

"Is that it?" he asked, motioning with one of his claw-tipped forelimbs.

Colin stepped closer and held the gym bag open for Verge to have a peek.

"This stays between you and me," Colin said, staring down through the cabin's front window meaningfully.

"It's something you don't want the boss to know about, huh?"

"It's not that I don't want Jolly Bill to know. I just don't see any need for him to know. This is a personal matter. This man was the best friend I had."

"As you wish. And I'm sorry about your pal and all, and I'm your pal, too, but time is a commodity. So is silence."

"I'll pay you what you need."

Colin then told Verge what had transpired at Club Feel only an hour earlier. "I don't know what this thing inside him was ... maybe some kind of virus he was infected with, that mutated him. But it seemed to me like it was something sentient, that wanted control of his body."

"Are you sure there's no trace of it still left in his head now?"

"No."

"Great. And you want me to do what exactly with this potential organic time bomb?"

"See what you can get out of his head that might tell me what led to this. See if you can access his memories. Tam's head is full of chips, and he's hardwired for the ultranet."

Verge's cockpit tilted forward as he looked down into the gym bag again. "So I gathered."

"If his memories aren't on a hard chip, you might follow a link to the ultranet where he stored his data on a nebula platform."

"I'll do what I can, but you'd better stick around while I do it. If that thing is still inside him, I'm going to want you here to cover my tail."

"Whatever you say."

Verge's insect-like prosthetic claws unfolded to reach down and lift the bag by its straps. As he turned to carry it toward his principal work area, he said, "And you just picked up his head right there in the middle of the dance floor and pranced out with it?"

"More or less."

"Aren't you afraid you were caught on security vid doing that? You might have every forcer and health agent in that precinct searching for you right now."

"I was just looking after my friend's remains, if they do find me. But I don't think they'd match my face to a record. I'm not stupid, Verge … I've never done time."

"Considering you're a guy who'll carry off a decapitated head in full view of dozens of witnesses, I'd say the fact that you've never been arrested has less to do with you being smart than it does with you being lucky."

"Whatever works."

Seated behind his array of control boards and monitor screens, Verge directed his vehicle's three slender arms to set the gym bag down on a work counter. Then, with something resembling reverence but more likely trepidation, he reached in and withdrew Tam Vonner's disembodied head, setting it down in the center of a glass scanner panel that was etched with a black graph-like pattern. Twisting around in his miniature chair, through his rear windows he saw that Colin had taken his pistol from its holster and held it at his side.

"Well, that's reassuring," Verge said. "Is that the same gun you killed him with?"

"What did you say?" Colin said.

"I ... " Verge faltered at the human's icy tone.

"I didn't kill my friend."

"Sorry, man. Sorry."

Verge returned his attention to the head, tilting it so as to examine the short stump of neck, displaying a cross-section as neat and bloodless as an illustration in an antiquated book of anatomy. The skin near the point of severance was a ring of silvery-gray, but the flesh there was not ragged, not even notched. Verge tapped the trachea with a gleaming claw. There was a clicking sound. The cross-section glistened as if it had varnished. "Check this out—the surface looks crystallized. I'm no biologist, especially when it comes to the human animal, but I'd say it's pretty obvious that thing didn't tear his head off. It's like it did something to just ... detach it."

The evenness of the neck stump made it a perfect base for Verge to rest Tam's head on. He tapped some keys at his cockpit consoles, and the graph-etched scanner panel glowed whitely.

"He doesn't just have chips inside," Verge announced, reading the scan findings on his screens. "He's got a whole computer in there—sacrificed a good chunk of his own brain for it. It's a Kessler V3. Runs off the bio-electricity of its owner ... who unfortunately in this case is dead. That means no power. But I think I can light it up myself. Anyway, your pal was serious about his craft. Why didn't you ever bring him into our family, man? He could've been doing all the same kinds of projects I do."

"He liked to keep it freelance," Colin answered. "He was afraid of the syndys. Besides, I didn't want to bring him in. I didn't want to damn him."

"Well look at us," Verge said. "The damned ... but still alive."

Refocusing on his work, Verge next produced three jacks attached to color-coded wires, and after examining the choice of ports in Tam's head, plugged the jacks into his skull. His claws danced over more keys. "For what it's worth," he announced, "we begin."

Two hours passed. Colin made no move to turn on Verge's VT to pass the time, and though there were some hardcopy books in the room he didn't touch them. He didn't even pace restlessly. He seated himself nearby and simply watched Verge work, quietly.

Throughout all the examinations and manipulations, Tam remained smiling unperturbedly, an expression so familiar to Colin that it was all he could do to look at the head. At the same time, he couldn't do anything *but* look at the head.

At last, Colin was jarred from his trance-like stillness by an exclamation from Verge, which translated into, "What the?" Whatever had surprised the salamander-like being, though, Colin couldn't say. What Verge saw was confined to his Lilliputian monitors, what he heard confined to the headset he had lowered over his ear holes. A minute later, Verge made a sound that was interpreted as a sigh, and his armature rose up straight on its tripod of legs and swiveled to face his guest.

"His brain tissue is compromised. Same as the neck: it's like the cells were crystallized. I can't extract anything that way. All his hardware is just as corrupted. The data's like a wooden house burned to cinders. But in the ash I did manage to find a few intact chunks ... jewelry and knickknacks, so to speak."

"Poetic. So to speak."

"My people prize poetry above all the arts."

"Just tell me about these fragments."

Verge conjured a large holographic screen for Colin's benefit. The border of the screen looked like gleaming metal, and Colin might have thought it was an actual physical monitor were it not floating in the air. Verge said, "I'm telling you, it's mostly just a few bits of flotsam and jetsam."

"Don't mix your metaphors. Get on with it."

"Okay." Verge started playing back the scraps of memory he had salvaged from the Kessler V3. "See what I mean?"

It looked like a vid taken with a camera, though it had been captured through Tam Vonner's eyes. The vid jumped a little, dissolved into digitized blocks several times, but what it plainly showed was a Siamese cat lying on a carpet, its blue eyes disgruntled and the tip of its tail flicking. And they heard Tam's voice, laughing. "You know I'm going out, don't you, baby? You always know when I'm going to leave you alone." He laughed again. "Stop looking at me like that … you're scaring me."

Colin said, "I remember her. That was Hetmet. She was in the family since Tam's mom was a kid. They kept that cat alive for fifty years … but she died like a dozen years ago."

The vid clip of the sulking cat ended abruptly, cutting off Tam's well-remembered laugh. In its place came a vid of a woman seen from the back, walking briskly, with her long green-dyed hair swaying. In the distance, above the low roofs of food stands, a triple ferris wheel turned against a bright blue sky. The surroundings indicated that Tam and the woman he was walking behind were at the annual Paxton Fair. She turned to smile at Tam over her shoulder, beaming a broad Choom smile at him.

"That was his girlfriend, Sool," Colin said. "He was crazy about her. She didn't feel quite the same. He never got over her."

Colin decided then that these weren't really just random flashes; they were souvenirs, representing things that Tam had loved, and had either consciously or unconsciously stored more securely in his supplemented memory. Locked in a safe that, though blackened outside, had survived the flames.

A dinner scene with Tam's parents cemented Colin's interpretation, but it only lasted a second before another switch. Colin's heart stuttered. Missra up close and dead center in the frame, thick curtains of wavy black hair framing her youthful face. Smiling straight at Tam, seeming to smile straight at Colin. "Tam, I can't believe you said that!" she said in feigned shock. Off-screen, Colin heard a familiar laugh. It was his own. Missra turned in profile, and Colin remembered the words before she said them: "Suck my ass, Colin."

"I wish," he knew he was going to say, but before he could hear his own words, another scene intruded with a noisy stab of static, as if badly spliced. This scene—the last in the chain—was very jittery and shot through with restless, infected areas of digital blocks. It appeared to be a first-person view of a stroll through a spacious library. The lighting was mellow, the aisles full of seemingly ancient books with leather spines and gold foil stamping.

Verge said, "If you were in here with me, you'd be getting olfactory sensations, too. Musty pages. It's all fake, though. That's a virtual library, but it's just a crumb. The library itself apparently resides on a nebula platform, but I'm not finding the link to get into it. Those books are actually files."

"Maybe that's the place Tam stored these memory fragments you salvaged."

"Keep watching."

This vid lasted longer than all the others put together. Tam continued up and down aisles, pausing to tilt his head to read titles. Colin read them, too. *Liber AL vel Legis* by Crowley. *De Furtivis Literarum Notis* by Porta. *Daemonolateria* by Remigius. *Kryptographik* by Thicknesses. *The Magus* by Barrett. *The Secret Lore of Magic* by Shah. *Books of Power* by Abdul-Kadir. *The Keys of Solomon* by Sargent. *Visions of Khroyd'hon* by Manly. *The Book of the Dominion of Mysteries*, *The Book of Night*, and *The Zhou Texts*. *The Metal Book* (which had hinged metal covers instead of leather), no author given. *The Book of Awe* by Marotta (which appeared to be triangular in shape). *The Veins of the Old Ones* by Skretuu, with its title in both English and Tikkihotto characters. The *Fizala*, its title both in English and Kalian characters. And the *Necronomicon*.

Colin muttered more to himself than to Verge, "This looks like the kind of dung Devon got Missra into."

Finally, Tam reached out and withdrew a bulky tome which on its spine read *The Atlas of Chaos*, by Wadoor, title and author's name printed in

English and also in the Choom language of Tam's people. Balancing it with difficulty in one hand, he cracked it open and turned pages with the other. Along with Tam, seemingly in real-time, Colin pondered strange geometric designs interspersed with the text, and bizarre, unsettling illustrations. One of these illustrations portrayed a Choom man in antiquated garb—a richly embroidered tunic and loose-fitting trousers—who was apparently contorted in agony as something like long slender tentacles emerged from his eyes, nostrils, and in more abundance from his hugely gaping Choom mouth.

As Colin studied this disturbing image, transfixed with recognition, the illustration appeared to move. The ink started to run off the page. But it wasn't ink. One of those tendrils in the drawing had detached itself from the man's eye socket, slithered quickly across the virtual paper like a worm, and onto Tam's right hand as it held the edge of the page. Tam cried out, and dropped the book to the floor, and the vid instantly deteriorated into blocks before the screen went blank.

Colin realized his breath had caught in his throat. His own right hand tingled, and he resisted wiping the back of it against his pants leg, lest Verge taunt him. Now he knew what it was that had caused Verge to exclaim, *"What the?"*

"I know," Verge said. "That's where it came from, isn't it? The thing that got inside your friend. Any idea what that was? Some kind of booby-trap? A virus that got into the Kessler? Though how a virus would turn into something seemingly organic—"

Colin cut him off. "So that's all, then?"

"I'll keep at it … see if I can restore the link to the actual library in the ultranet. But there's one more thing. I know you aren't a techie, but I'm sure even you know that everyone in the ultranet has a user handle. Your pal had contact information for hundreds of people, all under usernames, intact in a splinter of file."

"Physical addresses, too?"

"For many, not all."

"I want you to make a copy of that for me. Tell me the last few names he had contact with."

"All right … let's see." Verge consulted his cockpit monitors once more. "The last four contacts he had dealings with were LilBoyBlu, Mr. Gray, Pretty Kitty, and Miss Miss."

Colin nodded. "I'll want to go visit these people … see if any of them can tell me something."

"Any of those names mean anything to you?"

"Miss Miss," Colin said, looking away. "Her I know."

Verge copied the full contact list onto a wafer, which popped out of a slot in the front of his cabin. Colin pocketed it. In turn, Colin removed his cash card from his wallet, tapped a sum onto its touch screen, and inserted that into another slot in Verge's carriage.

"Why thank you, pal … very generous."

With the sum transferred, the card reemerged and Colin tucked it away. "Keep trying to clean up the link to that library, like you said." He took a step toward the door to leave, but paused.

He realized no one but the two of them knew that Tam Vonner was dead. With his body melted by Colin's own plasma, the only remaining evidence was his head. Someday, Colin determined, he'd tell Tam's parents himself. But not now.

"Do you need his head anymore?" he asked Verge.

"Nope. Anything I could use is in here now." He patted his main control panel.

In Verge's tech-crowded kitchen there was still a trash zapper. Colin picked up Tam's head from the scan panel, carried it back to the gaping gym bag, and set it down inside again gently, as if laying a newborn in its crib. Then he carried the gym bag to the trash zapper, opened its front hatch, lowered the bag inside, shut the hatch and punched the activate button. It lit up green.

Verge sighed. "Did you really need to do that in *my* place?"

This time Colin continued to the door, let himself out onto the balcony, and punched the button to summon the rickety elevator.

Clinging again to the outside of the cage was one of the glowing hardlight Screaming Pink Nazis. His jaw set, Colin pulled the Revenant from its holster and pointed it. Though the specter couldn't be harmed by conventional weapons, its programmed reaction was alarm, and it scrambled away out of sight like a spider.

Three
The Agony of Being

Early the next morning, while Colin's Razur idled at a traffic light—with streams of helicars directed by other means high above him, following invisible navigation beams on their commute to work—a huge hulking quadruped passed laboriously in front of him at the crosswalk. His first impression, though of course he'd never seen one, was a bison. He thought it must be a mutated animal, maybe even a dog, until he saw the bald human head protruding from the shaggy shoulders. Even from inside his hovercar, he could see the reddish hair that covered the mutant's body stirring with the swarms of parasites that infested its hide. The monk-like head looked grafted onto its body, the mutant's expression bland, as if it were fatalistic about its own unending suffering. One grew used to suffering, Colin thought, the way one was used to breathing. It was the nature of all Nature.

The shambling hulk made it to the other side of the street, the light changed, and Colin's hovercar floated forward again, gliding low over the pavement toward the apartment building where Devon Tellick lived.

Again he parked his vehicle at the curb, in front of a meter he slid his cash card into. Then he crossed to the apartment building, which was plated outside in faux copper sheets turned green with faux verdigris. The graffiti sprayed across the front door was authentic, however. In the gloomy lobby, smelling of mildewed carpet, he entered an elevator to find that new controls had been introduced, in keeping with the fad concern of Unreality Affliction. To request one's desired floor, one had to dial a number on a rotary dial. Then, to start the elevator cabin into motion, one was required to throw a large lever with a rubber handle. Colin sighed aloud, and programmed the lift for the fifth floor. It began to ascend.

The Third Musketeer, Tam had called Devon Tellick last night at Club Feel. First it had only been Colin and Tam, as adolescents. In their late teens, they'd encountered Devon. Where the connection between Colin and Tam had been their shared school and neighborhood, the connection between Devon and Tam had been their heightened proclivity for technology. But there had eventually been a Fourth Musketeer: Missra Sang, who had joined the group as Devon's girlfriend. When the couple finally broke up, Missra stayed on, having grown close to Colin and Tam. Especially close to Colin. They had soon become lovers. A few years later, though, connections had changed again. Missra and Devon had reunited. And that had been around the time that Colin had drifted away, leaving the others to become their own Three Musketeers.

If Colin hadn't seen Tam for a year, it had been more than that with Devon. But whereas Tam had made an effort to try to meet with Colin, Devon had not. Their friendship had never been the same since Missra had left Colin for Devon again. In actuality, their friendship had never been the same since Missra had come along in the first place. Colin had longed for the warmth of her eyes, the light of her smile, from the first day they had been introduced. It had been like another man having the sun all to himself, leaving Colin in darkness.

He walked down a dingy hallway lined with doors stenciled hugely with their apartment numbers, toward a door covered top to bottom with the red-stenciled label 8-E. Colin remembered it was a three-bedroom apartment, though of course Devon shared one of those with Missra. The other two provided more space for the abundant equipment that Devon utilized in his work creating holographic advertisements. Colin recalled 8-E as being almost as full of gear as Verge's flat, though Devon's freelance work had always been scrupulously legal—nothing like the work Verge did, nor even Tam's. Devon had always kept his nose clean.

Colin hesitated at the door to 8-E. Floating in place beside the stenciled door was a smallish holographic sign, glowing green, that read: FIAT LUX HOLO-DESIGNS. Devon had told his friends that "Fiat Lux" was Latin for "Let There Be Light." He had explained that rent was cheap in this building, as opposed to leasing office space in the Business District, for instance. Business had been steady, if not stellar.

At last, Colin pressed a buzzer below the hovering sign. No one responded. Devon hadn't responded to the calls Colin had made prior to coming here, either. He hadn't tried calling Missra, though she was the one he actually wanted to see, of course. She had been one of the last people to have contact with Tam. But Colin still wanted to speak with Devon, as well. The books he had seen in that chunk of vid Verge had salvaged were absolutely the kind of thing Devon had become obsessed with shortly before he and Colin had lost touch with each other. And Devon had instilled the same obsession in Missra. Maybe they would be able to make sense of what Tam's memory had revealed … the virtual black worm that had crawled off the page of that last book-file Tam had handled, and apparently infected him.

He stabbed the buzzer again, and held it. Still no answer. He was tempted to call Missra on his wrist comp, but couldn't bring himself to lift his arm, as if it suddenly weighed too much. He knew his reluctance was irrational. After all, he presently stood right outside her apartment door.

He decided to try Devon and Missra again later. For all he knew, they might have other employment now, no longer working at home. Maybe Fiat Lux no longer sufficed to pay the bills. Maybe, too, they'd decided to come out of their little Devon-Missra cave and forget their preoccupation with those old books, and what they believed the books concerned themselves with. Principally, that being the concept that a race of heterogeneous entities referred to as the Old Ones, so superior to humans they would appear as gods, threatened to shift into this dimension from some other dimension in which they—depending on the particular book and its translation/interpretation—slumbered or were imprisoned, or both. Whereas some people who delved into these books actually sought to aid these god-like beings in infiltrating and conquering this dimension, Devon and Missra had adopted the opposite stance: that such an occurrence should be prevented at all costs. They claimed the Earth Colonies weren't doing much to confront the threat, aside from covering up what they knew, and misrepresenting the occasional ominous occurrence.

Colin understood that part of the reason for Missra having become alienated from him was that he had scoffed at these notions of god-beings, dismissed her and Devon's fears as paranoia of an almost religious zealotry. He believed there was alien life of great power in the universe, barely understood, and there had indeed been various strange and controversial episodes in Punktown and on other worlds in the Earth Colonies network, but thinking of these alleged entities as *gods* ... gods that could be summoned or banished by reading passages from moldering books or by drawing geometric designs on a wall or floor ... to Colin it was like playing connect-the-dots with the stars, seeing anthropomorphic figures of deities where there was only the cold light of constellations.

"You live too close to the street to *see*," he remembered Missra having told him, in one of their arguments. She might as well have accused him of stupidity. Colin supposed it had been an easy choice for her, in the end, between Devon the do-gooder, the monster-fighter, and Colin the gangster.

He turned back down the hallway, reentered the elevator, dialed for the lobby and threw the lever again. He had that wafer in his wallet with the physical addresses of those other ultranet contacts whose usernames Verge had uncovered, but he'd decided to visit another person's apartment first.

Tam's.

In recent years Tam had lived a good distance across the vastness of Punktown from Devon Tellick, and the morning commute was still in effect. Colin wished Punktown had adopted a proposal to have artificial wormhole portals interspersed throughout the city, for traffic to make quick jumps from one major district to another, but it had been voted down as too costly. He recalled now there had even been protests, from what he deemed the lunatic fringe, about the possibility of malignant extradimensional life forms subverting the portals to their own purposes and using them to cross into Punktown. Devon and Missra had been against the portals, too, of course.

In any case, it was times like this that Colin thought he should get himself a helicar. The going was a little bit smoother in the air.

He finally arrived at Tam's apartment tower, and guided the Razur down into the building's multi-level basement garage. He watched suspiciously as a robotic limb on a ceiling track picked up his pretty hovercar to lift it into a slot above other vehicles, stacked to conserve space. Then, in the elevator—which thankfully had a holographic control panel—he tapped a virtual key for the thirtieth floor.

In his wallet Colin had an illegal skeleton key card, loaded with millions of random pass codes that could function on plenty of simple door locks. Though it was Tam, in fact, who had made the card for him, he knew Tam's own door would not be so easily hacked. Hacking wasn't necessary, though. The last time they had got together, before last night, Tam had given Colin a spare key card, telling him he could stay at his apartment if the need ever arose and Tam was out. Tam understood that in Colin's line of work, laying low in an apartment other than one's own might make the difference between life and death. Aside from the usual hostile rivals, one's own associates could turn into one's assassins at the slightest infraction.

Colin swiped the card across the reader beside Tam's door, there was a bleep, and the door slid open. Good; Tam hadn't changed the code since giving him the card. Colin stepped over the threshold, and the door slid shut again behind him. In the second it took for the door to close, he had his Revenant out to point the way.

He turned to look up behind him. On a shelf to either side of the door stood a metal canister that resembled a vase. Colin recognized them as security drones, but they hadn't been here the last time he'd been to Tam's place. If he had hacked his way in, the little robots would have levitated up from their shelves and come for him, with gun barrels probably emerging from those slots in their middles. Maybe they would have sprayed plastic riot bullets, or even the real thing. Colin was glad he hadn't had to find out which. Tam and his toys.

Colin noticed a number of green glass orbs set high into the walls here and there, too, that he didn't recall having been there before. Sensors? Cameras?

Though there were no windows in the flat, Tam had left a few lights on before heading out to the club; enough for Colin to see by. The cologne Tam had sprayed on before departing still hung in the air.

When he'd checked the entire apartment and discovered no obvious physical threats, besides the inert security drones, Colin put his handgun away and stood looking down at Tam's primary work center, the nucleus of his sprawling array of equipment. Though Tam was dead his gear lived on, subtly purring and whirring, lights still flicking on and off, virtual screens suspended in the air—some looking like solid monitors, others translucent and color-coded green or orange. Colin was hesitant to touch any of it, for fear of accidentally tampering with some important process, or even triggering those dozing robots after all. He raised his forearm and activated the wrist comp strapped to it, tapped out a number for Verge. After several moments, Verge's amphibian face filled the small screen. Colin wouldn't have known how tiny Verge was if he wasn't already familiar with his coworker's race.

"I got into my friend's place," Colin said. "I'm thinking you should come here and dig into his stuff."

"Sounds more straightforward than that impromptu autopsy I did last night," Verge agreed. "Of course, this house call won't be covered by last night's compensation, however generous it was."

"Just get here. You know you don't have to worry about that. Ready to take the address?"

"I've already traced your location. I can be there in an hour, if you want to do it now."

"I'll be here." Colin signed off and lowered his arm.

"What are you doing here, Colin? Where's Tam?"

Colin whirled around, startled, whipping out his pistol again, even though he had recognized the voice.

Missra Sang stood before him.

Four
Missra

Colin hadn't heard her enter the apartment, and the security robots hadn't stirred. Tam had apparently given her a key card, too.

"Is Tam here?" Missra repeated. "I was supposed to meet him today." She nodded at the Revenant. "What's with the gun, Colin?"

At first he couldn't reply, as he took her in. Missra—her dark hair cut short, her large doll-like eyes, the light dusting of freckles across her nose and cheeks, the sensitive pink of her full lips. Missra—barefoot, but wearing a tight black t-shirt, and similarly clingy black leggings that outlined the flare of her hips. Colin took the glimmering, star-like dots that sparkled across both articles of clothing as a mere effect of the material, not understanding it was more than that.

"You cut your hair," was all he could say at first. In all the time he'd known her, her black hair had been long, thick, and wavy. He had always pictured her hair first when conjuring her in his mind … remembered the feel and weight of it in his hands. And yet he liked this look. Her appearance still knifed him in the gut.

"I guess you haven't seen me in a while," she said. "I cut it some time ago."

"I guess it has been some time, then."

There was a thin gap between the bottom of her tight-fitting t-shirt and the waistband of her leggings, where the skin of her midriff peeked through. Colin tried not to look down toward it conspicuously, but he could still make out black markings around Missra's belly button. This was a tattoo of the Egyptian symbol called the Wedjat, or the Eye of Horus. Her navel formed the stylized eye's pupil. He knew, because he had kissed the center of that eye.

Missra glanced to left and right. "So ... Tam?"

"He's dead."

She snapped her eyes forward again. "Dead? What are you saying?"

"I'm sorry, Missra. I met him at a club last night ... Club Feel."

"He told me he was meeting you. Oh my God, Colin, tell me this is a joke. Tell me!" He saw her eyes quickly filling up, her lower lip quivering. He wanted to cross the few steps between them and embrace her, but he didn't. Couldn't.

"I'm sorry," he said.

"What happened?" she sobbed. "Was it something to do with you? People trying to kill you?" She was already prepared to accuse him. That stabbed him in the gut, too.

So he told her what had happened. He told her about taking Tam's head to his coworker Verge, and that Verge would be coming here shortly. He told Missra he'd been to her and Devon's apartment before coming to Tam's, but no one had been home. He had a habit of pacing when he talked at length—which he seldom did anyway—but throughout, Missra stood rooted in one spot, unblinking, until he had finished.

"This is my fault." She looked away, hugging herself tightly, by now quivering all over. "This is my fault, Colin."

"How is that?"

"That library your friend showed you, in Tam's memories. That's Devon's VR library. He won't give me access to it anymore, so Tam looked into it for me. I had Tam investigating whatever it is Devon has been up to lately."

"What do you mean? Are you saying ... did you two break it off again?" He hoped he didn't sound hopeful. Now was not the time for that.

She faced him again, tears streaming down her rumpled face. "Devon doesn't live at the old place anymore, though he still pays the rent. It's a place to keep me. He won't let me come with him to his new place, and I don't even know where it is. I heard someone buzzing at my door earlier … I didn't know it was you. Devon won't let me answer the door."

"What? Now what are you saying?" Colin said, grimacing in confusion. "Won't let you answer the door? What, is he keeping you a prisoner? Then how the hell did you get here now?"

"Devon is trying to make sure the Old Ones don't wake up, Colin. Wake up and cross over to our plane. He's immersed himself in that so completely, he's turned his back on Fiat Lux. He took out a huge business loan to buy up a whole bunch of new equipment that I thought he was going to install in our place, but it must all be at the new place, wherever that is."

"But why wouldn't he want you with him, to help him? You still believe in all that Old Ones dung, don't you?"

"It isn't *dung*, Colin. Yes, I still believe. And I wish I could help him, but he's too worried about me. He's shut me out, because he doesn't want anything bad to happen to me again."

"Again?"

"Don't make me tell you, Colin," she wept.

As a man who loved her, the worst scenario Colin imagined was that Missra had been raped. He could at least comprehend Devon's impulse to protect her, but he needed to know what it was that Devon had thought to protect her from. "Tell me," he snapped.

Missra appeared to draw in a deep breath. "Tam's not the only one who's dead."

"Stop talking like you're blasted on drugs!"

"Colin … I'm dead, too."

He blinked at her. Maybe it was drugs, after all, though he had only ever known Missra to smoke a little seaweed. Or had something snapped in her mind, with all these delusions about Old Ones? Was that why Devon was apparently keeping her isolated or even locked away at his old apartment, for her own safety? And if so, had she escaped from that confinement today?

But before he could try to articulate any of this, Missra continued, "You know what Devon does for a living, Colin ... at least, what he did until recently. Holo-advertising. Hardlight holos."

"Wait," Colin said. But he couldn't say more. He was getting it now.

"Devon recorded our memories, both of us, about a year ago. He was experimenting with coupling hardlight holos with complex AI intelligence. He was using us as models. But it was kind of a side project he tinkered with."

"Stop," Colin said. He had walked close to a wall, and leaned his forehead against it.

"When I was killed, he took the barebones AI he'd sketched of me, and fleshed it out in every way he could. He gave it all the memories he'd recorded from me. And memories are what we're made of."

"No," Colin whispered.

"I'm technically an AI, Colin. But I'm a perfect copy of myself. So perfect I can gain new memories. I can *learn*. I can be introduced to a new song and hate it or add it to my favorites. I can see a sad movie and cry. My thought patterns, my personality, are as they were when I was organic. That's the only difference, really. I'm just not organic anymore. But—"

"I told you to stop." Barely audible, but his voice broke. His eyes were wet and hot. He didn't want this thing to see his eyes like that.

"Colin." At last she stepped toward him, reached out, and touched his shoulder. Because she was a hardlight hologram, composed of photons bound into molecules to form a state of matter, Colin could actually feel her fingers on his body.

"*Don't touch me!*" he shouted, spinning around to blaze his glistening eyes at her.

Missra took a step back, lowering her outstretched arm slowly. Her cheeks were still wet. Or at least, gave the illusion of being wet. "I'm sorry, Colin."

"When I find Devon, I'm going to kill him."

"Why would you say that?"

"What, are you afraid I'll do it? Do you think you still love him? Do you think you actually feel anything?"

Missra nodded. "Yes. I know I do."

"I'm going to kill him for getting Missra killed. I know it's him who got her killed—wasn't it?"

Missra sighed, lowered her eyes, and he knew it was true. "Devon wanted a very rare book for his ultranet library—*The Atlas of Chaos*, written hundreds of years ago by a Choom named Wadoor. Wadoor understood there's a web of lines and angles and curves that permeates everything, and interconnects every dimension. He discovered formulae that allow a being to travel along the pathways of this network, mentally or even physically. Devon already owned a similar book written later by a Tikkihotto named Skretuu, called *The Veins of the Old Ones*, based on Wadoor's ideas, but he wanted the Wadoor book, too. Not only for his own research, but to take it out of circulation so the wrong people wouldn't get their hands on it." When Colin didn't interrupt her, absorbing her words, she continued. "Devon learned of a small group of Tikkihottos, living in an old decommissioned pollution sucker in the neighborhood of Willow Tree, who supposedly owned a copy of Wadoor's book. He made contact with them over the ultranet ... but he was wary. He wanted to get a feel for why they'd have a book like that. When he talked with them through u-mail, they sounded like they had the same attitudes we had. It sounded like they had the book to use it against those who worship the Old Ones and hope to resurrect them. The Tikkihottos told Devon they couldn't sell him the book, but they'd let him borrow it and copy it."

"It was a trap," Colin murmured. "They were getting a feel for you, too. They knew you were the enemy."

Missra went on, "We went to meet them in Willow Tree. Devon, me, and a friend of ours you wouldn't know—Orson. Orson was a mutant. Big, scary. Orson had a gun. The Tikkihottos met us. Maybe they would have attacked us right away if they hadn't seen what Orson looked like. I think that threw them off. Three of them met us ... there were three more hidden inside the pollution sucker. They brought us inside, and they even let Devon handle the book. Then, Orson saw something that tipped him off … we don't know what it was. But he pulled his gun out, and then it was gunfire all around."

"When did all this happen?"

"Eight months ago."

"Four months after your memory recording. So how do you remember any of this?"

"I don't. Devon told me. Anyway … Devon got outside to our car with the book."

"He left you to die inside?"

"I was already dead. He saw me die."

"He left your body there with them?"

"What could he do, Colin? I was dead."

"And Orson?"

"The last Devon saw, Orson had been hit badly a few times, but he was still fighting to cover Devon's escape. Devon said Orson killed a couple of them."

"But he didn't wait to see if Orson might get out of there alive?"

Missra shook her head. "No. He felt Orson wasn't going to make it. And Devon didn't have a gun."

"I see. Did he call the forcers after that?"

"No. He didn't go to the authorities. The war against the Old Ones and their cults is fought in the shadows, Colin."

"And so he started making you after that. To pretend he hadn't got you killed."

"Because he missed me. Because he loved me." The AI's voice actually sounded hurt, and angry.

"*Me*," he echoed, laughing, his eyes looking a little crazed. "You aren't a 'me.' You're a blasting videogame character!"

"I'm telling you, Colin, I'm not just a replica of Missra. Except physically, I *am* Missra."

"Except *physically*? Yeah … right … and a virtual globe is a planet. Except physically."

"I know you aren't this ignorant of tech … it's just that it's me that's making it hard to accept."

"I accept things, all right. I accept that Devon made you as a souvenir. You're a talking headstone. He made you out of guilt for bringing you into his little crusade and getting you killed."

"I know who I am."

"You *think* you do."

"Talking with me now, do you feel like you're talking to Missra? The Missra you've always known?"

"At best, I feel like I'm talking to a ghost." He turned his face from her.

"Maybe it just boils down to the fact that you can't fuck my body now," Missra said.

Colin looked back at her sharply. That had, in fact, sounded like Missra. The pained heat in her eyes, now … how many times he had seen that there. Put that there.

"But some people do fuck hardlight holos," she said, a sickly bitter smile coming to her lips.

"Is that what Devon does?" Colin said. "Oh, that's right, he turned his back on you, like Frankenstein did to his creation." Then, Colin's expression changed and he looked around him. "So … so how are you able to travel to Tam's place?"

Missra pointed to one of those green glass orbs set high in the walls, that Colin had noticed earlier. "Devon let Tam install holo-emitters in his place and link them to his system, so I could visit him. So I wouldn't feel alone when he was away. Later on I guessed he did that because he knew he was going to leave me behind. I think if it gets to the point where he can't pay the rent on the old place anymore, he figures I can stay with Tam. But now … now Tam is gone."

"He won't let you answer the door to your old apartment?"

"No … he's blocked my access to door functions. And he made my access to the ultranet limited, so I couldn't contact anyone. He wanted to keep me safe. And he didn't want anyone to find out about me, and then find out how I died. That was why I depended on Tam to find Devon for me, and see what he's doing with all that new gear of his, wherever it's set up. Because I couldn't look for Devon on my own. I guess you're right in that sense, about me being a prisoner. A ghost who can't affect her surroundings."

"You don't know where Devon is physically, but Tam found him in the ultranet?"

"Yes."

"And got into his library."

"Yes. And from what you saw of Tam's memories, it's the current library—not a cache. Because he has Wadoor's book recorded in there now as a file."

"So what was it in that file that got into Tam and infected him?"

"I can't say. A spell? Maybe being Choom himself, being able to read Choom writing without artificial translation, had something to do with it. Maybe he was speaking an incantation aloud to himself as he read it, or even just reciting it mentally. Or maybe it's something else ... something that developed when Devon scanned the book into a file. Some kind of corruption ... something that was activated or made manifest."

"I watched the recording through Tam's eyes. His virtual eyes. Afterwards, I felt a tingling in my hand, like I'd had an electric shock. For all I know, those worm things are growing inside me, now, too."

Missra stared at him silently.

"My friend is dead and I want answers," he said. "I don't want maybes."

"I can only guess."

"That isn't good enough," Colin hissed. "I want to talk with Devon. So you can't contact him?"

"I try, but he won't answer me."

"Then when Verge is here, I'll have him get inside Tam's system, find Devon in the ultranet, and I'll get to him that way."

"You can try. That doesn't mean he'll talk to you, either. But ... last

42

night Tam said he'd found out some new things. He was going to tell me about it today."

"Maybe it was just that he'd hacked into the library, seen that Wadoor book, and that worm crawled onto his hand."

"It could have been that."

"Verge gave me the usernames of some people Tam had contact with in the last days he was alive. One of them was yours. I thought you said Devon gave you no ultranet access."

"Only to contact him and Tam. Most times I'd message Tam to see if he was home before coming over. Instead of just dropping in, in case he was busy."

"The other usernames were LilBoyBlu, Mr. Gray, and Pretty Kitty. Do you know any of those people? Is one of them Devon?"

"I don't recognize any of them. And Devon wouldn't reply to Tam's messages, ever since he moved out of my place a couple months ago."

Colin lowered his head, slowly wagged it. "I can't believe Tam knew about you, sat right across from me, and didn't tell me."

"I'd ordered him not to, Colin. I meant to tell you someday. I guess it's someday."

He sighed. The sigh felt like he was expelling his spirit, leaving only the empty husk of his body. "Devon made you out of guilt, and then he abandoned you out of guilt. Because he couldn't face you anymore."

His wrist comp beeped. He raised it closer to his face, opened its channel, and saw Verge on the screen again. "I'm here," the albino newt said. "Ready to let me in?"

"Yes. Come up." Colin lowered his arm.

"I'll be going," Missra said.

"You don't want to watch? See what we find out?"

"You can fill me in later."

"You're still afraid of being found out. Afraid of contact with outsiders. Don't you see? You're following Devon's programming. You don't have free will."

Missra stared at him in silence again, and then she turned away and walked toward the apartment's closed door, padding barefoot. Before she reached it, though, she was gone.

Maybe part of him had still held on to the hope that this was all a vengeful joke, a trick, a ruse, but seeing Missra simply blink out of existence brought the reality of her loss home with the decisive turn of a vise's handle, and his heart in the vise's jaws.

Missra ... gone.

Five
Dead Man's Face

"Hey," Verge said, when his own mobile work center stood over Tam's central work station, "where your friend is dead, can I have some of this stuff?"

"No," Colin said.

"I'll pay you something, of course."

"No. Get to it. First, can you find out who he pays his rent to, and if it's up to date?"

Verge used one of his robotic claws to pull a cord out of the front of his cabin, which he jacked directly into Tam's system. Within a minute he reported, "Rent paid for this month, but due again in two weeks."

"Send a payment." Colin handed over his cash card.

"Why do you want to pay his rent?"

"Just do it."

Colin pulled up Tam's chair and seated himself, while Verge leaned over physical and holographic control consoles on his tripod legs.

"What next?" Verge asked.

"I want to find out where a man named Devon Tellick lives. Not the address where he runs his company Fiat Lux; I know that one. He has a new one."

"Did your friend know the address? Will it be in his system?"

"No, he didn't know it, but maybe you'll have better luck. Also, see if you can find the link to that virtual library we saw in Tam's memory. It belongs to Tellick."

"How'd you find that out?"

"You ask too many questions. And try to establish contact with Tellick through his u-mail. If you get him, turn it over to me."

"That everything?"

"No. I want to know if those usernames you gave me have any bearing on what happened to Tam. LilBoyBlu, Mr. Gray, and Pretty Kitty."

"There was another one."

"I told you, I know that person."

"Okay, well, where to start with all this?"

"Maybe while you do your thing, I'll contact those three people, if I can, and see what they're about. But they don't know me, and maybe they won't talk. Can you make it look like it's Tam calling?"

"Sure, we can do something like that."

Verge went to look for Tam's saved u-mails, sent and received, but immediately came up against a wall. "Huh—he's got his logs locked up. This boy was into heavy security."

"You're telling me," Colin said, glancing behind him at those two dormant security drones.

"I was going to open a sent message from your friend, and use his likeness from that. Tell you what—you have a u-mail account, caveman? You use the ultranet, or just the plain old net?"

"I'm not into that whole immersive VR dung, but yeah, I do have an ultranet account."

"I'm astonished. Okay, open your own account. You have any saved messages from your guy?"

"Yeah … give me a minute."

Verge copied Tam's recorded likeness from the message to Colin—the one in which he had initially invited Colin out to Club Feel. He then removed the sound of Tam's voice. "You'll speak while this is playing," Verge explained. "I'll pollute the sound with a bit of static and garble to hide your voice. They'll think it's just a glitchy connection. And I'll distort the image, too, so they won't see the lip movements aren't matching up.

Crude, but it should pass."

Colin opened a drawer in Tam's desk and found a little plastic box filled with thin, disposable ultranet interface disks. He peeled off the backing from two of them and pressed the adhesive side to both his temples. Verge tapped a couple of keys, and Colin found himself bobbing on the flat placid surface of the ultranet. It was the depths of that ocean he didn't care for. They were limitless, and could get dark. One could drown down there.

First, Colin put out an ultranet call to the person whose handle was Mr. Gray. He was prepared to leave a message, but soon enough a live person answered. To Colin's mind's eye, it was as though the man were sitting in a chair facing him in the flesh. He almost flinched back from the man's intense face. He was a Kalian. Like the Choom, Tikkihottos, and Sinanese, one of the few nonEarth races to closely resemble humans. The man's flesh was ashy gray, the whole of his eyes black, and his head was wrapped in a turban of metallic blue material.

"Mr. Vonner?" he said, sounding confused and perhaps leery.

Colin knew Tam's stolen image was fluttery, and interrupted occasionally by breaking down into digital blocks. He hoped "Mr. Gray" didn't ask himself why a tech wizard of Tam's caliber couldn't manage a clear signal.

"Yes," Colin replied in his distorted voice. "I just wanted to check in with you."

"About?"

"Are you, uh, satisfied with my work?"

"Yes, yes ... as I told you, you confirmed my suspicions that my wretched wife was showing her hair to another man."

Traditional Kalian women were required to wear blue turbans themselves outside the home, only allowing their lustrous long hair to be uncovered in the presence of their husbands. Their hair was considered to be the epitome of carnality. The expression "showing one's hair," though, implied hair of an even more personal nature.

Gray went on, "She has been dealt with harshly, as she deserved. Not only will she not show her hair again, she won't ever want to show her punished face in public. As for her lover ... he too will know my righteous anger. But I will seek the services of someone else for that."

"Uh, okay," Colin said. He wondered how Tam had proven to this man's satisfaction his wife's infidelity. "Like I said, just wanted to check in with you. If you need anything else from me, I'm here."

"Again, I thank you."

As soon as Gray signed off, Verge said, "I found it."

Colin swiveled his chair. "Found what?"

"Your friend sneaked a cam into her lover's apartment. No ... no ... it looks like he found a way to spy on them right through the guy's comp monitor." Colin couldn't see what it was Verge was watching on his screens inside his miniature cabin. "Oh ... wow."

"What is it?"

"Tam must have liked what he saw. Oh yeah ... yeah ... humans aren't my thing—maybe if you had sexy tails—but I like what I see, too. Well, it isn't what I'm seeing ... it's what I'm feeling."

"What are you going on about?"

"Tam used the vid he shot of Mrs. Gray and her lover and turned it into a fully sensory sim memory for his own use. There's a VR template you can buy for that, you know—plug in whatever lover you want."

"I wouldn't know. I like the real thing."

"You wouldn't know the difference. Don't believe me? Over to you." Verge tapped a keypad.

Suddenly a new face materialized in front of Colin's own, only inches away this time. The face of a beautiful gray-skinned Kalian woman with her eyes closed, her mouth gasping open, her long black hair spread wide across a mattress. Colin could feel her hot breath panting against his face. Could feel her hands on his back, the insides of her thighs against the outside of his thighs, her belly pressed beneath his own, her tropical interior. He smelled her skin, which had a natural scent like patchouli or sandalwood. "*Taaam*," she moaned.

"Stop it," Colin said, as if to the woman.

"Want me to send a copy of this to your account?" Verge purred somewhere unseen beside him, like a voyeur to Colin's lovemaking.

"I said stop it," Colin growled, as he felt himself not only growing hard, but hitching closer to ejaculation.

"You are one cold fish, Rex," Verge said.

Mrs. Gray was gone, Colin once again facing only an incomprehensible jumble of computer equipment, and a hard shudder went through his body. "Don't pull that on me again," he said breathlessly.

"Not my fault if your pal was lonely and horny. Too bad he apparently got that poor beauty sliced up or doused with acid."

Colin was, in fact, surprised Tam would have taken on a dirty little surveillance job like that, like some low-rent hired detective. He must have been scraping a bit to stay on top of his bills.

He said, "Let's just move on to the next one. I'm going to try LilBoyBlu."

"Go to it. I'm still trying to find this Tellick person you want to track down. Tell me, is this someone you plan to kill—knowing you?"

Colin said, "He got two people I loved killed."

"Enough said," Verge grunted.

Colin put out another call, this to the handle LilBoyBlu. He let the u-call ring and ring. After several minutes he was ready to break off and try Pretty Kitty instead, when finally his call was answered. Again, Colin almost drew back in his chair. It was not just because he disliked the persuasive reality of the ultranet—it was because this new person was of such a fearsome appearance.

Sixteen years ago, the so-called Blue War on the extradimensional planet called Sinan had ended. In that conflict, the Earth Colonies had fought in support of the Jin Haa people as they sought independence from the Ha Jiin majority. In addition to sending in Colonial Forces, the military had created a large force of clones custom-designed for Sinan's jungles of entirely blue foliage. After the war had ended, most of these surviving clones had been recruited for hard labor on the most far-flung colonies, but others had utilized their military training and superior physical traits by becoming security guards, bodyguards to the rich, and the like.

LilBoyBlu was one of these former Blue War clones. They had all been produced from only a few master templates, this one having the features of a man of African descent. Like all Blue War clones, though, he was entirely hairless, his blue-pigmented face and head covered in camouflage patches of varying shades of blue. His whole body would be the same. Now Colin understood the clone's username, though it seemed a bit too whimsical when looking into his smoldering eyes.

"Vonner," the clone snarled. "I was trying to reach you all morning."

"Sorry," Colin said. "I've been away."

"Yeah? I think you were hiding from me, you momfuck Chew-'em."

"Why would I be doing that? I'm the one who just contacted you, remember? I'm returning your call."

"Then did you hear the messages I left?"

"Just run it by me again."

"You hear that screaming behind me?"

Colin did. It sounded like a man wailing as he was being tortured. Colin knew what that sounded like, from experience. "What's going on?"

"All innocent, huh, Vonner? You didn't sneak a virus into those programs you gave us?"

"I don't work that way. Why would I?"

"Maybe you know somebody who doesn't like us over here, who paid you to corrupt our stuff."

"I don't know any enemies of yours. What kind of virus are we talking about?"

"That's what we want to know!" the clone shouted, spraying spit. Colin instinctively blinked. "My man Nichts, here, says there's something in those combat programs you hacked from the CF. We all opened them up for a look, but one of my men—Cero—was a pilot in the war. He's chip-implanted. He uploaded a flight program straight to his head. Now he's the one you hear screaming back there in the other room. Not only that … he's got *things* inside him. You can see them moving around under his skin!"

50

Colin glanced at Verge beside him, then back at the clone who seemingly sat right in front of him. He could smell cigar smoke on the man's clothes. "What day was it, again, that I sent you those programs?"

The clone told him. It had been early the previous week. The man went on, "And I'm not feeling so great myself, Vonner ... none of us are. Killer headaches, seeing things out of the corner of our eyes—weird things. We hear weird sounds. I want answers, while you're still alive to give them!"

"Maybe ... " Colin stalled while the ramifications bubbled in his brain " ... maybe it's something the Colonial Forces puts in their files as a booby-trap in case they get hacked, and I wasn't aware. Like, hardlight nanomites that attack the user's body?"

"Yeah, could be. Or could be some trick you put in there, like I say. Virus or virtual nanomites, or both. All I know is, you sold us poisoned product and I want our systems cleaned up. Our tech, and our bodies."

"I'll ... look, I'll have to sort this out on my end, then I'll get back to you."

"Get back to me? When?" the clone bellowed. "When all of us here are going crazy and tearing at our skin like Cero? If you can't fix this fast, Vonner, I will hunt you down and *end* you!"

Tam's already ended, Colin thought.

"I found a business profile for LilBoyBlu," Verge said quietly beside him. "His name's Jornel Riggs. At least, that's the name he legally took on after the war. Was a sergeant in the CF. Runs a security company called Ronin Security, but their ad reads more like a mercenary outfit to me."

"Who's that with you?" Jornel Riggs demanded.

"Just my partner, trying to help me figure out your problem."

"I heard my name."

"Try to calm down so we can work this out together."

"Sir." Colin overheard a voice speaking urgently beside Riggs—he had his own Verge, apparently, the man he'd called Nichts—though Colin couldn't see the speaker. "That isn't Tam Vonner. It's a mask."

"What?" Riggs roared. "What is this?" Suddenly he was rocketing up from his seat and lunging forward. Reaching his hands out to Colin's face, as if to tear the flesh from his skull.

Adrenaline shot through Colin Rex. His instinctive response was to defend himself, and counterattack. His primal self told him this attack was real, and as a result, it was as though strong hands had gripped his ankles and pulled him quickly down below the surface of the ultranet. Deep down.

Somehow he felt the clone's hands close on the mask Verge had made of Tam's face. It exploded into drifting and dissolving digital blocks, like blown dandelion seeds. It wasn't pain Colin had felt, and he wouldn't know how to describe the sensation, but it was profoundly unpleasant.

Then he was thrusting out his own arms, and shoving Jornel Riggs away from him. He could feel the contact of his hands against the clone's rock-solid chest. Off balance, Riggs fell against his chair and both toppled backwards. Riggs blurted out a cry, but it was cut off as Colin ripped the sticky interface disks from his temples.

He looked again to Verge, drawing in deep breaths to regain his composure. He felt as if he'd burst suddenly awake from a nightmare. "Did Tam sell them those combat programs after his visit to Devon Tellick's library?"

"I didn't get a date stamp on that library memory," Verge replied, "but it has to be. I'd bet you anything he was in that library sometime before he gave these freaks their war games stuff. It's obvious—whatever virus Tam picked up, it infected the product he gave Ronin Security. And it may not be a coincidence that this man Cero got hit harder than the others, the same way Tam picked up the virus in his own body. Tam had that big Kessler implant in his head. Hardware in the brain must make one more vulnerable. That's why you and me and these other clones haven't grown anything nasty inside our bodies."

"*Yet*," Colin said. "Well, this isn't good. These guys are mad, and they don't know who we are, which makes them madder. I hope they don't know where Tam lives and try coming over here." It wasn't that he feared for his own safety, but if the mercs damaged Tam's equipment, this apartment might no longer serve as a safe haven for the Missra AI. And if Devon stopped paying the rent on his old apartment, then where would the AI reside? Trapped like a genie in a bottle in some computer wherever Devon was now?

"If the stuff Tam sold to Ronin is compromised," Verge mused, "I wonder how much of the rest of his tech and programs have been infected. Even a caveman like you knows what viruses love to do."

"Spread," said Colin. "All right, look, I'm going to try Pretty Kitty next. If this person had some work done, too, after Tam picked up the infection … " He let his words trail off ominously.

"Let me check for a business profile on that username, before you go in," Verge said. Only moments later he had it, and opened a large holographic screen in the air for Colin to see the results.

"Is that … "

"Yep, it's an ad for a sim porn site. Hm … 'twenty munits a minute for a full sensory experience.'" Verge chuckled. "Your buddy sure had his appetites. Let me take you to the site itself."

"Forget it," Colin said. "If that's all it was."

"Afraid to get too heated up again?"

"You'll be feeling heated up when I treat you to a plasma bullet."

"My pal Colin," Verge laughed nervously, "always the joker."

"Why don't you copy whatever data you need, or can access anyway, and take it home to work on? I have other things to do today and I can't leave you here alone."

"Afraid I'll steal some of Tam's toys? I wouldn't do that without your okay."

"A wise attitude. But that isn't my concern. What I'm thinking about is those angry blue men from Ronin Security."

"Oh," said Verge. "Right. It's possible their guy Nichts will track down this address even if Tam has defenses against that. Then again, if Nichts was as good as Tam they wouldn't have needed Tam to steal that military software, whatever it was. Anyway, I'd rather not be here in case they do come around."

"A wise attitude," Colin repeated.

Six
Kitty at Play

Colin Rex liked to change his residence from time to time, jumping all across Punktown, to keep potential enemies guessing about where to corner him. Or maybe it was some kind of restlessness he didn't care to examine closely. In any case, he had been at his current apartment for five months. (Maybe another month and it would be time for a new place.) Though it would have been agreeable to his personality to rent a whole floor in a retired industrial building, or some similarly desolate structure, he preferred places that were full of people. Less chance of being attacked in a heavily populated location.

This current flat was in Subtown, the subterranean sector of Punktown, which though expansive didn't cover nearly as much area as the city above. The apartment building was built from riveted metal that looked like blackened pewter. Actually, this building didn't stop short of Subtown's ceiling—which was crisscrossed with a weave of joists, power cables, water and sewer pipes—as most of the buildings down below did. Instead, it pierced the ceiling and continued on up into the open city, where the building proved itself to be a support column in an elevated section of highway. Several of the other legs of this stretch of highway were similarly hollow, similarly occupied. Immense as the city was, there was always the need to find more room in which to house its ever-growing population. Sometimes improvisation was the key.

Once inside his flat, Colin bolted the thick metal hatch that served as his door, removed his jacket and draped it over the back of a kitchen chair, and stepped down into his sunken living room area. The interior walls of his flat were like blackened pewter, too.

Colin didn't have computer hardware spread throughout his apartment, like Tam and especially Verge; it was confined to one smallish desk in a corner. His principal monitor and the system unit were both built into a box-like case of polished cherry-red wood, the keys of his physical keyboard looking like they'd been shaped from translucent amber. This was because, most often, his system merely served a decorative purpose.

Colin seated himself before his system, and from an old mints container extracted his only pair of reusable and seldom used interface disks, which he stuck to his temples. He prodded a key to activate a voice-operated search. "Username Pretty Kitty," he said.

He had given his computer a female voice, soft and soothing—like Missra's. The voice replied, "Primary result is an ultranet link, Mr. Rex. Shall I take you to the foyer?"

"Take me."

A black wall seemed to rise up in front of his face, and everything peripheral to that turned depthless black as well. His apartment was flooded out of view by the inkiness. The forward wall turned out to be black velvet curtains, which parted, and a woman slipped through them into a ray of light with no source. She was Sinanese, exquisitely beautiful, small in stature, both delicate and tough-looking as her people tended to be, with robin's egg blue skin and waist-length black hair that shimmered with slippery light. She wore a black corset so shiny it looked wet, which constricted her already tiny waist, elbow-length rubbery black gloves, and thigh-high black boots with platform heels that gave her something more like adult height. Colin had never cared for S&M type accoutrements, much less S&M play, but apparently Tam had felt differently.

He was prepared to converse with Pretty Kitty through her ultranet avatar, but when she spoke he realized she was just a recording, however intently she fixed her eyes on his. She purred, "Welcome ... I've been expecting you. Step inside Kitty's den." Her full-lipped mouth spread in a carnal smile. "Don't make me make you." She turned and slid between the black curtains again. After hesitating a moment, Colin stepped after her. He told himself that even this recorded construct might be able to answer questions about customers like Tam, or preferably put him in touch with an actual sim porn worker—if there *was* an actual Pretty Kitty. He rationalized that maybe Tam hadn't been merely a customer; perhaps he had done work for this person, even set up her ultranet site for her.

Colin didn't want to admit to himself that he was curious to see what a person experienced in here. He might not care for S&M, but he had nothing against Sinanese women.

He had been feeling poisoned in every last cell of his body, every cell of his soul, since meeting Missra's construct. He felt like an unsheathed dagger. All this quivering tension resided behind his reserved mask. Sometimes when he felt this way (though had he ever felt *this* way?), he went to visit one of his syndy's numerous prosties. He wasn't one for imaginary flesh, but right now he crackled with a violent need for some kind of release.

He divided the curtains with his hands, ducked through them.

And stepped into a bedroom. The curtains behind him were gone as soon as he'd passed between them.

Pretty Kitty was gone, too.

Colin looked down at his body. It wasn't as though this were his first excursion into the deepest depths of the ultranet (he was now standing on the ocean's floor, as it were), but it never failed to unsettle him that he could hear the slightest rasp of his foot against the floor if he shifted it, could feel the air parting against his hand if he were to sweep it in front of him. He saw he was wearing the same clothes he was wearing back in his apartment. Who had made that choice? His subconscious?

As in his apartment, he had taken off his black suit jacket but still wore his pistol holster clipped to his belt. He touched the handle of the Revenant, its coarse checkered grips. Reassured by that familiar sensation, he raised his head to concentrate on his surroundings.

The New God

The bedroom Colin now stood in so solidly was as red as it was spacious. The deep red wallpaper was flocked to give it the texture of velour, overlaid with a grid-like design of glinting gold. The wall-to-wall carpet was a darker red, embroidered with a similar gold grid pattern. The tent-like draperies that enclosed the massive canopy bed were velvety red.

The ornate carving of the canopy bed's posts, and of the white-painted fireplace, gave the room a touch of the Victorian. Huge mirrors within flowery gilt frames were spaced along the walls, making the room look even larger, reflecting one inside the other, gold grid within gold grid within gold grid in an intricate web receding into infinity. The high ceiling, glossy white, bore raised lines that sectioned it into panels, forming yet another grid.

But the room's balance of the lurid and the austere was tainted ... corrupted. The bed's heavy curtains looked dusty and frayed. The mirrors were smeary, cracked, loose shards having fallen to the soiled and greasy carpet. The fireplace's maw was heaped with black ash that had overflowed onto the carpet, which was scorched in that area. He could smell the charring. Questionable fragments were mixed in with the ash. Broken birch branches? Bits of shattered white crockery?

But Colin was focused on the room's walls. The wallpaper was mildewed (he could smell that, too), making the velour seem more like fuzzy mold. It was peeling, sloughing away in swathes, baring large areas of the bone-like plaster beneath. And on these exposed white areas, someone had painted words, apparently using their fingers. The red-brown medium the words had been rendered in could only be dried blood.

He read one urgent bit of graffiti, turned his head to study another, and another.

The first read: THE WEB IS GROWING. IT IS ALIVE.

Below that, probably added later: A STRAND PASSES THROUGH ME. I'M JUST ONE BEAD.

Next, in sloppy big letters: MORGELLONS ARE REPLACING MY INSIDES.

Then, in small tight letters: THEY ARE HERE. THEY HAVE ALWAYS BEEN HERE. THEY ARE GONE NOW BUT THEY WILL BE BACK AND YET THEY ARE STILL HERE.

And: IT IS ALL IN ONE. YOG-SOTHOTH CTHULHU SHUB-NIGGURATH Y'GOLONAC UGGHIUTU OTHERS.

Under that: YOGSOTHULUBNIGGOLOCUTU

Finally: YOGTHUTU

This couldn't be right, Colin thought. This decay was beyond decadent ambiance. Tam could not have been excited by such an environment, no matter what activities he had kept from his old friend.

Having turned in a full circle to read all the graffiti, Colin finally registered the most disquieting detail about the room.

There was no door.

Movement at the corner of his eye caused him to jerk his head to face the bed again. The red velvet drapes were stirring. And then, a leg pushed its way out between the folds. The leg wore a thigh-high black boot with a platform heel. The foot alighted on the carpet, and a body followed, slipping between the red curtains just as the recorded construct had appeared from the black curtains in the site's foyer. This entity partly resembled that previous figure ... but in other ways it was radically different.

When it had both feet on the floor, it stood upright and faced him, and Colin put his hand on the butt of his gun.

The legs were the one feature shared with the recorded version of Pretty Kitty. But from the thighs up, this figure was mostly a twitchy chaos of flickering static. A fluttering wraith that seemed to be struggling valiantly to achieve corporeality. Bits and pieces of the entity briefly attained something like solid form: a smooth blue shoulder, a slender left arm wearing a long rubbery glove, the upper curves of breasts pressed up by the corset. Yet each fragment would become lost again in the seething visual disturbance, with another fragment solidifying elsewhere. The face remained a blank mask of static, but black hair swam in the air above the apparition with life of its own, myriad long strands writhing and coiling like a nest of serpents.

The right arm ended in a long tentacle formed of gritty, sparkling static, that trailed across the floor. Colin realized it was a whip in Pretty Kitty's fist.

The figure took one jerking step toward him. The movement was like watching an old celluloid film with a series of frames edited out, badly spliced back together.

Colin drew the Revenant from its holster and let it hang by his leg.

With the next stuttering step forward, Pretty Kitty began speaking. Her voice was like two voices playing one on top of the other. One was the same voice he had heard in the foyer. The other was much deeper, guttural and rasping.

One voice asked him, "Have you come to play with Kitty?"

Below that, the shadowing voice garbled something that sounded like: "*Ph-AN gloo-ee …*"

"Take my hand, lover." The left arm, a pseudopod of static, extended toward him.

"*… ma-gluw NAF …*"

"Before the cock crows, let the two of us become one flesh."

"*… ka THOOL hoo …*"

"Don't look so nervous, handsome."

"*… ra UL yay …*"

"You'd better stay back," Colin said in a calm voice that nevertheless had the quality of a rattlesnake's clatter.

Kitty ignored him, taking a third juddering step toward him, and said, "Come pet Kitty."

"*… wuh-gaah NAA gul …*"

"Make me purr."

"*… fah TAAG an.*"

Pretty Kitty was clearly not in her right state of mind. She'd become infected, like Tam. But Tam had become dangerous, and Colin had had to destroy him, and this woman wasn't his best friend. He raised his handgun and pointed it at her. He didn't know if she could hurt him in this place …

or if his virtual bullets could hurt her. He'd heard of people who died in the ultranet, and as a result died in real life as well—from heart failure, or an aneurism. Or simply from *believing* too much, maybe? He wasn't willing to risk that she couldn't do him harm. He said to her, "I told you to stop. I don't want to hurt you."

"Ahh," she said in both voices simultaneously, one sensuous and the other a growl, "but *we* want to hurt *you*." And to emphasize her words, she cracked that whip of static that blended into her right arm like a tentacle. Sparks leapt from its tip.

"Computer," Colin called out. He took a step backwards. "End connection."

The connection hadn't ended.

Pretty Kitty took another step toward him. "Who are you talking to, lover? There's only you and me here." She lashed her whip again, the loud snap like a gunshot, and sparks spattered to the carpet. "And those inside me."

"Computer!" Colin shouted.

Then, for just a second, Pretty Kitty's mask of static fell away, and what Colin saw was a raw red face with only black sockets for eyes, and a wide lipless grin, but then the static returned. And yet another step forward.

Colin lowered his gun a little to point it at her right knee, and started to squeeze the trigger.

Before he could discharge his weapon, however, Pretty Kitty pitched forward abruptly as if she'd been tripped or lost her balance on her dizzying heels. She fell onto her face with a hard thud, only a few feet from his toes. Her long hair splayed limp around her head, no longer alive and swirling.

Colin kept his gun trained on her warily, but she no longer moved or spoke. The static continued flickering. Finally, as he stared at her, he noticed something else. Blood was spreading under Pretty Kitty's motionless head, glistening red soaking into the red carpet.

As if the pooling blood were a signal, or as if his computer had finally heard his command, the red bedroom fell away like toppled stage scenery, revealing his apartment waiting behind it.

The New God

He was sitting at his desk again. The first thing he checked was that the Revenant wasn't in his hand. He was almost surprised, though relieved, to see that it was still in its holster.

He couldn't peel off the interface disks, or stand up and move away from his handsome computer, quickly enough.

Seven
Read All About It

"I know you were shy about it and all, but it wasn't smart looking into Pretty Kitty on your own," Verge told Colin with a touch of smug amusement the next morning, when Colin returned to his apartment. "Even with your friend Tam's safeguards, look what happened to him. Course, it caught him by surprise. My system shouldn't let anything nasty through the barriers, since I know to be on the lookout, but you … heh. Your best bet at this point is to trash your whole setup. I'll fix you up with a new system, stronger and safer … at a reasonable savings, of course."

"Is that why you called me over here? To sell me a new computer?"

"I have things to show you. You *are* paying me to look into things, aren't you?"

"I am. A lot. So show me."

Last night, Colin had called Verge on his wrist comp—wary about using his computer again—to let him know what had transpired. Verge had since looked further into Pretty Kitty, and what he revealed to Colin now on a virtual screen was a story from the morning edition of Punktown's largest newspaper. Verge related the relevant details as Colin leaned in to read the article for himself.

Verge said, "Last night a sim porn worker named Stella Cybula, who went by the handle Pretty Kitty, was found dead by her daughter, who lived with her."

"She was forty-seven," Colin noted. "And an Earther ... not Sinanese." There was a photo of Stella Cybula's fleshy, boozy face, framed with platinum-dyed curls.

"At first it looked like foul play, but then the forcers determined the woman's wounds were self-inflicted," said Verge. "Her daughter reported her mother had been acting increasingly strange over the past few days. She thought maybe her mom, a former addict, was using again."

Colin found a list of self-inflicted injuries in the article. Cybula had gouged out her own eyes, but had been able to interact with the ultranet via the disks pasted to her temples. She had also cut off her own ears, and flayed the flesh from the lower half of her face. Colin recalled the brief glimpse he had had of Pretty Kitty's red wet face beneath the static. She had deeply excised her nipples, and mutilated her genitals.

He said, "She must have died right there and then, when I was with her."

"Blood loss," Verge said. "She'd written all kinds of things on the walls of her apartment in her blood."

The article didn't relate what those things painted on the walls had said, but Colin was certain they were the same words he had seen in the virtual boudoir.

"Anyway," Colin said, straightening up as Verge collapsed the screen, "all this confirms to us is that anyone Tam contacted through his compromised system, after his visit to Devon's library, could be affected by that virus-thing."

"And they in turn could spread the infection on to other people they have contact with. Actually, you're probably lucky you have a bare bones computer. This lady's system was pretty good, in service of her occupation. Just as having hardware in your head apparently magnifies the virus's impact, I'll bet having a more powerful computer does the same. I haven't seen the thing knocking at my door, yet, but you can believe I'm on my guard."

"I don't feel possessed at the moment," Colin said.

"Let's keep it that way," said the tiny albino creature. "Leave the tech work to me. You should stick to the rough stuff. Okay, next item of business.

You know I copied some of Tam's data while I was at his apartment, but I also established a link while I was there so I can access some of his system right here from my place. And therefore, I was finally able to get into his u-mail."

"Yeah? And have you found anything that would point us to where Devon Tellick lives?"

"Not yet. Remember, you're the one who told me this Missra friend of yours tasked Tam with finding out where Tellick is. So we're not exactly going to find an address already waiting there for us, are we?"

"So is there anything of interest to us in Tam's system?"

"Well, I did find the link to the nebula platform where Tellick stored that library Tam broke into."

"You did? "

Inside his cockpit, Verge held up one tiny paw-like hand. "But wait. The platform was empty—cleared out. Tellick must have realized someone was snooping around in there, and he moved the library altogether. Wherever it is now, who can say?"

"Dung," Colin cursed.

"But I've been looking more into Tellick, and I found out he used to work as a researcher for a company called Daedalus Data … before he went into business for himself with Fiat Lux."

"I already know that," Colin said.

"Yeah? Well, looking into Daedalus a little I found a funny news story from about two months ago."

"Funny how?"

Once again, a virtual screen was called up. Another article from an earlier edition of the same Punktown newspaper. This article's headline read: BRAZEN THEFT AT DAEDALUS DATA.

"Brazen isn't what was stolen," Verge said. "Just to let you know."

"Don't fuck with me," Colin said as he started reading.

There was no night shift at Daedalus Data, and even the security guard at the front desk went home after the employees had all departed for the evening. After hours, an intruder had somehow gained entrance to the facility without tripping any alarms, perhaps having obtained an employee's access code or ID. The intruder had walked out with two pieces of expensive equipment.

"So?" Colin said. "Why is this even news?" Surely Punktown supplied countless more lurid stories, such as the demise of Stella Cybula, to entertain the newspaper's readers.

Verge sighed, and scrolled down. "Look at these images captured from the security vid."

The first still image from the recording—taken in the building's front lobby—showed the front of a very tall, very broad figure wearing a trench coat and a fedora, its wide brim pulled low to shadow his face except for a square pale jaw. The person's arms hung loose by his sides. He was moving across the carpet past the unattended security desk. The second image showed the same figure from the back, on the way out again, approaching the glass door. Now, under each arm this person carried a bulky piece of equipment that Colin couldn't begin to identify.

Verge explained, "Those are two Gibster 800 cryo-cooled encephalon comps." Encephalon computers, even Colin knew, were based on bioengineered human brain tissue. "Daedalus was using them in research, to power state-of-the-art holo-emitters. Those Gibsters are so powerful, the researchers were bragging that they could use them to project a hardlight house of multiple floors that people could actually live in."

"Interesting. And?"

"Well, Fiat Lux, right? Your old pal Tellick made his living from designing hardlight holos."

"So, are you suggesting that person—" Colin pointed at the figure in the trench coat and wide-brimmed hat "—is Devon?"

"If that is Tellick, he must be pretty damn strong. Those Gibsters probably weigh five hundred pounds apiece."

Colin snapped his head around to study the image again. "Huh."

"A mutant, maybe?" Verge suggested.

"But you're thinking … "

"I don't know what I'm thinking. You know Tellick, not me. But I just thought it was funny … Daedalus Data. A theft of two super comps from a place Tellick used to work at, around the time you say he left his old apartment for new digs. Who knows?"

"Well that's definitely not him, but it's something to bear in mind," Colin said. He faced the tiny being's glassed-in cabin again. "All right, now—new mission."

"You know, I do actually have other work to attend to. You remember our boss Jolly Bill, don't you? Do you realize that 'jolly' part is a bit of a misnomer? A joke, as it were?"

Colin ignored him. "This is all I want from you now. I want you to get inside Devon's old apartment."

"Bound to be tricky."

Because he didn't want to omit any more information that might be of use in Verge's endeavors, Colin had reluctantly admitted to him that Missra Sang had been murdered by a cult of Tikkihottos who had been living in a decommissioned pollution sucker in the neighborhood called Willow Tree, and that she now existed only as an AI construct that was limited in its capabilities. Though this construct could travel freely between Devon's former apartment and Tam's, it was prohibited from admitting callers into either man's flat.

Verge continued, "You know those drones in Tam's place? Tellick might have something like that, or worse. Someone with his skills isn't going to make it easy to get inside his inner sanctum, even if it's his old inner sanctum."

"Do it remotely if you're able. If not, just go over there and see what you can do."

"If I meddle with his door, for all I know I could trigger an explosion. Maybe not, if Devon's afraid to see all his gear destroyed. But maybe in the case of intruders he *would* want all his gear destroyed."

"He wouldn't want to see Missra's AI destroyed, if it was important enough for him to create in the first place."

"I'm sure he can make Missra available to him where he is currently, whether he chooses to allow her access to that place or not."

"I didn't say don't be careful, I'm just saying try. If we're going to find anything useful on Tellick, that's the best place to look."

"Oh? So then why was Missra, who lives there—so to speak—not able to find out where Tellick is now?"

"You can get into Devon's system where the AI can't, and that might produce arrows. Again, maybe the AI's programming limitations prevent it from seeing some things that will be right under your nose. And speaking of the AI ... " Colin hesitated a moment, as if he almost thought better of going on, but he did " ... is it possible to set up equipment in my apartment, holo-emitters like in Tam's place, so it can come to my flat too if it wants?"

"Well, I'll bet wherever Tellick is, he still monitors Missra. He'd probably see if we tried that, and stop us."

"Good. Maybe that would flush him out."

"Yeah. Or, it might make him put the Missra AI on ice, to thwart us. Are you willing to risk that?"

Colin dropped his gaze.

"I didn't think so. You loved that girl ... I can tell."

"Don't say any more," Colin warned, in a voice that Verge knew to take seriously. "I'm just ... I'm just concerned about accessing the AI for information in the future, now that Tellick has left that place and Tam is dead."

"I understand," Verge said carefully. "Maybe that's a project for later on, then, after you've found Tellick and ... and done whatever it is you plan on doing."

"Get on it," Colin said, moving toward the apartment's door.

"And what are you up to, now?"

"Something I can't put off anymore," Colin said without looking back. "You just stick to the tech work. I'll handle the rough stuff."

Eight
Pollution Sucker

With the construction several decades ago of the great "air factory" off Route Forty—outside the core of the city—tasked with drawing pollutants out of the air, Punktown's former fleet of airborne "pollution suckers" had been put into retirement. There had been different models of pollution suckers, varying in size from small house to offshore oil rig, but all of them had floated in the sky over the city—either hovering stationary in problem areas, or making their rounds like roaming sharks. Some were fully automated, others manned by robots or even organic crews. Now they were a thing of the past, seen either as quaint or crude relics. They had mostly been scrapped, though it had been trendy for a few years for the upper-middleclass to rent apartments in some of the larger specimens, grounded and converted to that purpose.

The pollution sucker in Willow Tree was in the midsized range, and though it had been used for shelter, it had not been formally remodeled. It rested on the cracked and weedy parking lot of a closed-down factory. It was covered in graffiti, and brittle dead vines reached up from the pavement to entwine its lower parts. It looked like a huge, complex engine that had been dislodged from some aircraft and plummeted here to rest on this desolate plot in a neighborhood of Punktown that seemed more bleak, more morosely subdued, more melancholy than most.

Colin Rex parked his Razur several streets over, and walked casually to the shuttered old factory and the pollution sucker in its parking lot, as if taking a leisurely stroll through a pleasant neighborhood.

Within sight of the grounded pollution sucker, Colin came upon three young boys sitting on the sidewalk, bent over a banged-up portable vidgame player. They looked up at him cautiously. One of them was a mutant with a large, grayish translucent skull that had a deep depression in one side, within which a set of teeth was clenched in a grimace. Even the air factory couldn't get all the toxins out of Punktown's atmosphere.

"Hey," Colin said laconically, standing over them and nodding toward the pollution sucker. "I knew some folks who used to live in that thing. You know if they're still there?"

"Yeah," said the mutated boy. When he spoke, the extra set of teeth in the side of his head gnashed together. "Some Tikkihottos live there."

"Mm, okay," Colin said. "You guys might want to go play somewhere else. I don't think it's too safe right around here."

The boys, even at such a young age well acquainted with the ways of Punktown, without question scooped up their toy and scurried off down the sidewalk, away from the pollution sucker. Colin continued strolling toward it.

As he neared the derelict craft he saw that at least two dusty-looking hovercars, one battered hovertruck, and a hoverbike were parked on the far side of it. The front of the dark machine, though, facing toward the sidewalk, was clear of anything but strewn trash and broken bottles. Colin removed a card from his jacket pocket as he crossed toward the front hatch, which was rimmed with heavy rivets. It was the skeleton key card Tam had once made for him.

Colin swept the card in front of a reader beside the hatch. A red light blinked orange, uncertainly, for several seconds. Colin thought the card wasn't going to suffice, and that he'd have to find another way in. But then the light turned green at last, and he heard a loud *thunk*. He regretted the metallic clunk, but at least he was in. He turned the door's lever, pushed the squealing hatch inward, and stepped over the threshold into a chilly gloom that smelled of grease and incense.

As he closed the hatch again behind him, he slid the Revenant free of its holster.

Light bars were set into channels in the low ceiling and metal walls, but a third of them had burnt out and another third flickered wanly in their death throes. Gauges with motionless needles were set into walls beside monitors that showed only static or were black and dead. The floor was made of grated metal panels that could be lifted out to get at pipes and cables beneath.

As Colin crept down this first narrow corridor, labeled metal doors started to appear along its length. Some of them were closed, though others stood open or had been taken off their hinges, leaving only empty doorways. He peeked into the rooms beyond warily, but only saw crowded machinery, work stations with more dead or offline computers.

He moved down an off-branching corridor, following the smell of incense. Below that scent, and the grease, was a growing stink like spoiled meat. It wasn't quite the taint of a dead and decaying body; Colin knew that smell. At least, not a human body.

This corridor ended in a right angle, but just before that was an open doorway, and Colin poked his head and his gun inside to find it was the pollution sucker's old crew quarters, with bunk beds recessed into three of its walls. On the bottom bed of one of these, a Tikkihotto male lay napping. Colin might have mistaken him for a fellow Earth human were it not for his translucent eye tendrils, which lay spilled motionlessly on his pillow.

He stepped into the room. Atop a small chest of drawers in a corner, close to the Tikkihotto's head, rested a few empty cans of Zub beer, a hardcopy pornographic magazine, and a sheathed dagger. Colin could tell by the dagger's scabbard and its handle bound thickly in blue and orange thread that it was a traditional Tikkihotto weapon.

With floating steps, he moved closer to the bunk bed. A single glassy eye filament raised itself up alertly, turning like a periscope to point at him.

Colin set his gun down on the chest of drawers, in the same motion drew the long spike-like blade of the dagger out of its sheath. More filaments rose up and swarmed, agitated, and the Tikkihotto's head started to rise from its pillow, but Colin brought the spike blade down in his fist and buried it to the grip in one mass of tendrils. The head fell back on the pillow, the tip of the blade having emerged from the rear of the skull. The filaments whipped in a mad spasm for a moment, then shivered, then flopped limp and unmoving.

Colin saw a cheap shotgun with a pistol grip lying across the top bunk. He took it down and flicked on its readout, saw it was loaded with five shells, each containing eight balls of crystal shot, that shattered against bone to tear the body with bright shrapnel. He returned his own gun to its holster, racked the shotgun's slide, and left the sleeping quarters.

He stole around the bend in the corridor.

The walls of this corridor, between the doors that lined it and even across a couple of the closed doors, had been tagged with luminous green and purple graffiti. Had gang kids partied inside the pollution sucker before the Tikkihotto cult claimed it? But then as Colin approached the nearest bit of tagging, he saw that the graffiti was in the complex hieroglyphic-like language of the Tikkihottos, which often overlapped layers of text and colors, some of which only they could see. In fact, Colin had the vague impression there was a third ghostly pigment sprayed on the walls, that just eluded him. That would probably be the color they called "shrain." Colin imagined that if Tam were here right now, with that Kessler implanted in his head, he'd be able to read and translate these words or phrases. To Colin, it was just the visual equivalent of speaking in tongues. Nevertheless, though this graffiti was in a different language and medium, he was weirdly put in mind of the graffiti he had seen in Pretty Kitty's dream den.

He heard a hissing sound ahead of him, maybe steam erupting around one of the valves that sprouted mushroom-like from the pipes that meandered like subterranean roots along the walls and ceiling. He also saw a fluttering bluish light emanating through an open doorway just ahead. He peered around its edge.

It was the largest work station he had yet encountered, perhaps the pollution sucker's main control center. Three chairs stood before three long counters supporting a complex amalgamation of equipment. The hissing came from small monitors built into the consoles, but also virtual screens floating above the work stations. Most of these screens displayed only grainy snow, but several shared the same vid or broadcast. This vid looked as though it might have been shot underwater, a close-up view of some kind of thin silver sea plants, thousands of dense squirming strands. But they weren't all waving in the same direction, as they would with a current. Each flexible stalk moved on its own, reminding Colin of the eye tendrils of the Tikkihotto themselves. Furthermore, these silver strands contorted and coiled in such a way that he could almost swear they were trying to form letters in some language, arduously spelling out words like a planchette on a Ouija board.

He suddenly looked away from the large virtual screen he had been staring at as if mesmerized. The backs of his eyes had begun to burn.

Anyway, there were other features in the room that demanded his attention.

Here and there on shelves and on the work counters and even atop computer gear, fat white candles burned on tea saucers or in ash trays, their light lapping at the walls. The air was faintly hazy with incense sticks jutting up from an old coffee can that had been filled with dirt. And on the floor of the room, geometric patterns had been rendered in great arcs and circles and in slicing angles, with symbols painted at the points of intersection as if to label them. These patterns had been painted in glowing green, purple, and apparently shrain.

Yet the main feature that demanded Colin's attention was a Tikkihotto man lounging back in one of the chairs in front of the control panels, washed in the guttering bluish light. He looked to be napping, but on closer inspection he was trembling all over as if a powerful electrical current ran through the chair he was slumped in. The true cause of his quaking was no mystery, though. The Tikkihotto man had disposable ultranet interface disks stuck to his temples. And stuck to his forehead. And all across his bare, shaven head. And across his bare chest, even pasted over his nipples. He wore only boxers, soaked with urine. His optical tentacles contorted and coiled in the air. Colin believed they were trying to emulate the motion of the silver worm-like strands on the monitors … trying to spell out an alien language, maybe in some sort of response to their message.

The Tikkihotto quivering in the chair was oblivious to Colin as he stepped into the room, and looked around him.

Physical books overflowed a shelf built into the wall above one work station, reminding Colin of the tome Devon, Missra, and their friend Orson had come to acquire from the Tikkihottos eight months earlier: *The Atlas of Chaos*, by the Choom author Wadoor. The book that, in scanned replica, Tam had handled in Devon's virtual library … the book from which the viral force or influence had emerged.

Colin approached the shelf and ran his eyes over the spines, most of which, if they bore lettering, presented just as much gibberish to him whether they were in English or not. He thought that before he left this place, he should destroy all these volumes, lest they come into someone else's possession. He was not admitting to believing in what Devon and Missra believed, only that it was best to deny access to them for other deluded souls who might do harm in the name of such beliefs.

One book had been removed from the shelf and lay on the work counter below, resting open to pages of Tikkihotto text again, so complicated and layered it almost gave him a headache to look at it. Was this a copy of that other book Missra had mentioned, the one by the Tikkihotto author Skretuu, who had followed in the footsteps of Wadoor? Colin recalled the title: *The Veins of the Old Ones*. He transferred the shotgun to one hand so he could close the book and look for a title on the cover.

He found the book had been crudely covered in a new binding, seemingly of leather, which had been brushed with something like thick glistening varnish to preserve it. The effect made the binding look old, though that wasn't the case. There was no title, only a symbol, that appeared to be tattooed onto the leather rather than printed or painted there. This black symbol was what the Egyptians had called the Wedjat, also known as the Eye of Horus.

Where the eye's pupil should have been was a funny wrinkly flaw in the leather, like a scar. But Colin knew that it was a navel, because he had used to press his lips to that navel.

"Hey!" said a voice from the doorway behind him.

Colin spun around and fired the combat shotgun at the same time.

A Tikkihotto man went flying backwards out of the doorway, his back slamming into the opposite wall of the corridor. Colin marched toward him, stood over him pointing the weapon. The eight crystal spheres had caved in the front of the man's chest, the white ends of shattered ribs poking out like fangs in a ragged red mouth.

"Uhh," he heard the Tikkihotto in the chair in the control room moan, like a sleeper suffering a bad dream.

Colin returned to the room, but stayed back a safe distance as he blasted the shotgun again, and again, continuing until he had exhausted its shells. Then he cast it aside to clunk against the floor. His ears rang from the enclosed detonations. It wasn't the Tikkihotto he had blasted, however, but the computer equipment that ringed the control center. Sparks leaped like incandescent grasshoppers from smashed monitor screens and system units. All the virtual screens had evaporated.

Colin jerked his pistol out of its holster, grabbed the seated Tikkihotto by the neck and jammed the Revenant's muzzle into his cheek. Through clenched jaws, Colin said, "Do you hear me, momfuck?"

"Yeah … yes," the Tikkihotto moaned, tendrils whipping around in wild disorientation.

"How many of you are in this cult?"

"We are widespread. Across worlds and dimensions … "

The gun muzzle ground against the Tikkihotto's teeth through his squashed flesh. "I mean in this pollution sucker."

"There are four of us."

"My friend told me there were six."

"Two of us were killed."

"Eight months ago? By a big mutant?"

"Yes."

Missra's friend Orson had managed to bring down a few of them, at least. But that left one more cultist Colin needed to account for. The noise would have alerted him … he might have already fled.

"Let me go back inside," the Tikkihotto slurred, as if drunk. "Let me *commune.*"

Colin glanced up briefly at one remaining active monitor directly in front of the man: the field of rooted worms signing their unfathomable code. "What are those things?" he demanded through gritted teeth.

"The cellular units that compose the whole, across all time and all space," the Tikkihotto said rhapsodically. "The cells that compose the Old Ones. Summoned here to unite us all. The infidel will be used for his meat. The faithful will be rewarded with *communion*. And it will all be the same—we will all be the same—united in glorious chaos!"

Colin had no use for rhapsodies, only hard facts. He discharged the Revenant against the man's face. A projectile of solid metal blew the back of the Tikkihotto's shaven skull off in a large, almost neat circle, like the lid lifted off a teapot.

Then, pulling back, Colin thumbed a key on his handgun to change over to .55 plasma gel capsules. He pointed the Revenant at the end of his arm, and triggered it repeatedly. First he shot the book bound in the skin of Missra Sang. Then he raised his arm a bit and fired at the shelf crammed full of books. Green plasma spread hungrily, with an almost sentient lust to undo everything it touched, glowing with terrifying beauty, fat gobs of it dripping down to eat into the work counter below, doing further damage to the sizzling, spitting equipment.

Colin stepped back out into the corridor to go in search of the last cultist, only to find that the cultist had been seeking him out as well.

The figure lurching, shambling down the corridor toward him had once been a Tikkihotto, but had been distorted, deformed, and not at birth like the mutant child Colin had met outside. He knew this person had been altered in something like the way Tam had changed ... through the influence of a more enigmatic form of pollution.

This was the source of the stench of spoiled meat, suddenly so strong it made Colin clench up his lungs. Spoiled meat perhaps with the green stink of advanced infection.

The transfigured being had grown so wide and tall with its deformities that it nearly brushed both walls and the ceiling too. It was naked, and bulged with unevenly distributed, glossy and blackening growths like great sarcomas. One arm was merely a thick, shapeless club of fleshy bubbles, one dragging bloated leg like a tree trunk. Its optical tentacles had grown much longer, much thicker, like Medusa bundles of snakes sprouting from its skull, nearly taking up the whole of its face. They strained toward Colin, reaching out as if to seize him.

Colin saw a few ultranet ports in the sides of the thing's skull, such as Tam had possessed, leaking viscous silver fluid.

Colin fired the Revenant. The gel bullet burst against the hulk's chest, releasing its fast-spreading luminous green blanket. Noxious smoke arose and Colin almost gagged, closed off his throat again. The thing blurted a snuffling noise from whatever mouth it still possessed beneath its face of tentacles. It kept loping toward him. Faster, in fact.

Colin backed off several steps down the corridor and fired again. This capsule struck the abomination in its face of serpentine limbs.

The tentacles started to melt and drip, shrivel and shorten to stumps. As the plasma spread back to the Tikkihotto's head, it began to eat into the front of its face, making one great orifice of its optical sockets and nasal passage and mouth. And yet it still came limping at Colin, making an unearthly gurgling sound as the plasma slid a molten path down its throat.

Colin fired his pistol three times in rapid succession, striking the transmogrified Tikkihotto high in the chest twice. The third bullet plunged into the crater it had for a face.

At last, it toppled forward like a felled tree, landing on its front with a thunderous splat. The plasma hissed and sizzled, and the billowing fumes began to obscure the spectacle of total dissolution. Colin could hold his breath no longer. His eyes watering, he turned around and retraced his path to the pollution sucker's entrance.

Punktown's air had never tasted so sweet. The playing boys were nowhere in sight, but Colin guessed they were hiding somewhere not too distant, spying curiously.

He had parked his Razur across the street from an old stone bridge of native Choom design, that now supported an elevated stretch of hovertrain repulsor track. As Colin began to slide into the driver's seat, he saw that in his absence an expensive black hovercar had crashed into one of the arched bridge's supports, crumpling in its nose. A male of Earth ancestry in an executive's five-piece business suit had disembarked from the car, seemingly oblivious to his broken and bleeding nose, and stood spray-painting graffiti on the stone flank of the bridge.

He was writing the word YOGTHUTU.

Nine
Camouflage

Missra didn't need to sleep so as to rest or recharge, but now and then she let herself go inert for a period if only to pass some hours. She had been allowed enough access to the regular net to view films and read virtual books, but sometimes these diversions were not enough to engage her interest. Or at least, to engage her feelings.

Her *feelings*. What would Colin say to that statement, if she were to vocalize it to him?

Colin.

Since she had chanced upon him in Tam's apartment, she had already returned there almost a dozen times in the hopes of finding him present again. She told herself it was to see if he had learned any more about where Devon was, what he was up to, and how Tam had ended up the way he had. She told herself those were the reasons.

She padded barefoot from room to room, as if stalking Tam and Colin, feeling the absence of both men like a blade in the center of her chest. And Devon, too. Their old group, shattered now like a dropped glass sphere, once so perfect. Two of them dead—including herself.

She presently stood in Tam's bedroom, taking in the mundane details of his life. Of his last day. Dirty clothes he had later meant to gather and clean, a mug half-filled with Choom mustard drink on the bedside table, gone cold. The bed was unmade. Imagining her friend walking back into the room after his night at the club with Colin, from which he had never returned, Missra felt her chest tighten, tears swell in her eyes. And what would Colin say to *that* if he saw her tears … if she told him of the tightness in her chest? Would he only say that she had no eyes, had no chest?

On a shelf Tam had arrayed a set of toy action figures from a movie series he'd been enthusiastic about. She'd teased him about his boyishness. She reached out to pick one figure up, and because it was small and light she was able to do so, turning it this way and that to examine it before replacing it. She touched a button on a bureau and the top drawer slid out, revealing badly folded underwear and socks. She prodded another button, this one on the bedside table, and a large drawer slid out from under the bed, startling her and making her jump back. In this coffin-like drawer lay a diminutive young Asian with large breasts straining against her white blouse. She wore a black school blazer and short plaid skirt. One might think it was a dead body Tam had preserved and stashed away, but the eyes opened and stared up at Missra blankly.

"I never knew Tam had anything like you," Missra said to the pleasure android.

The automaton didn't respond. Tam has probably programmed her himself, only to respond to him.

Missra said to the android, "Poor lonely Tam." And then: "I suppose if someone was able to implant my persona into your head, then Colin would like me better, huh? A tangible body he could touch. Something he might be able to wrap his brute brain around." As she said this, her eyes felt hot and wet again. She punched the button on the bedside table, and the drawer slid back into place.

"Dung," she hissed to herself. "Grow up, Missra. You're still as messed up and confused now as you were when you were alive."

Funny—for a long time she hadn't thought of herself as being dead, only restricted in her abilities, compromised in her freedom. Not until Colin had come along again.

She decided to return to Devon's old flat, maybe to watch another movie. Maybe to go inert for a while. One of these days, she thought, she might just go inert and never become active again. Maybe it would be better that way. Maybe that was the way things had been meant to be all along, and Devon had arrogantly interfered with her destiny. Devon raising the dead, summoning ghosts, playing god. She wondered, was he so unlike the spell-casting cultists he considered their enemy?

Thoughts of returning to Devon's place (could she really think of it as her place—did she truly *have* a place—could water call the cup that held it its home?) caused her to wander to the door to Tam's apartment. As if, instead of willing herself to shift from one flat to the other, she might go through that door, down to the street, and hail a cab. She stared at the key controls beside the door panel. Stared as if she had never seen such a device before. As if it were far too complex for her to even begin to fathom. She started to lift an arm, one finger extended, to push a button … any button, until she discovered the right one to open the door or at least, for a start, to unlock it … but her arm froze in the air before her. She stood that way a long time, as though mesmerized or distracted by some inner thought. As though she were hesitating, reluctant to go through with her movement.

But she knew it was that she *couldn't* go through with the movement. She could not will her arm, her finger, forward any farther. It was as if she had stepped up against an invisible force field.

It wasn't that she needed to punch in a code to unlock and open Tam's door—not from the inside, at least. It was not that she had been denied some special security clearance. It was simply against her programming. Her intention was not allowed. She could not will her actions around or through the barricade that Devon had made in her virtual mind. That was the real locked door.

Missra lowered her arm slowly, back to her side, and this time pride prevented her eyes from tearing up. But she was glad that Colin had not seen her vain struggle just now. It would have only confirmed his accusation. That she was not Missra.

Before she could turn away from the door, it opened. As it began to do so, she flinched back, startled. Had she managed to touch one of the keys after all, without being conscious of it, and the response had been delayed? Had she somehow influenced the door controls with her mind, connected as she was with Tam's home system, however tenuously?

But as the door opened, four men pushed into the room, men with blue flesh and blue camouflage patches swarming across their bald heads and intense faces. The men had a variety of guns in their hands, and their eyes were all trained on her like laser beams as she quickly backed away from them, into the center of the room.

The man in the lead, who wore a hooded coat, started to demand, "Who are—"

Nichts, the one who had overridden the lock outside to let them in, spun around and started to warn, "Sir—"

The robot drones that had been resting like metal vases on their shelves to either side of the door had already taken to the air, slots opening in their smooth surfaces and gun barrels extending. Even as the gun barrels appeared, they started firing streams of projectiles.

The blue man closest to the door leapt back out into the hallway again. Two others dove to the left and right, spinning and turning their own guns toward the hovering drones. The hooded blue man, who had begun to speak to Missra, charged at her. She backed away some more.

"Call them off or die!" he roared at her as he came.

She wanted to protest that the levitating little robots were not under her command.

The blue man who had jumped to the right fired his weapon at the drone floating nearest to him. He held a two-fisted compact assault engine, a Blue War model called an AE-93 Sturm, also patterned with blue camouflage, which from its multiple muzzles could discharge a variety of ammunition, shotgun pellets, mini rockets, plus ray bolts. He released a segmented line of the latter at the drone, but the red energy bolts glanced off, leaving only scorch marks. With the flick of a thumb he was firing a fully automatic chatter of solid bullets instead. These jacketed slugs punched through the canister and the drone wobbled in the air. But before it collided blindly with a wall and then thumped dead and smoking to the floor, a stream of its own projectiles strafed the front of the blue man who had killed it, exploding across his chest and face. He immediately dropped the Sturm, covered his face in both hands and screamed, slamming back against a wall. The projectiles were capsules like those that contained corrosive plasma, but these instead contained a nonlethal pink glowing gel that nonetheless spread like plasma and gave the sensation of burning, though no tissue damage would occur.

The blue man who had leapt to the left, Nichts, opened fire on the other drone with his pistol but he too was struck by a number of the robot's riot capsules, and he also howled, doubling over and shielding his face too late as the pink gel seemingly cooked his eyeballs.

As he folded up, one of Nichts' stray bullets struck Missra.

She said, "Uhh," and jolted a little, as the bullet passed through her belly and out her back. She looked down and saw a spray of black digital blocks, sparkling as if with tiny stars, jump out from her body, but they were immediately sucked right back into her.

A split second later, the leader of the cloned soldiers, Jornel Riggs, had his arm around her neck. He swung himself behind her and tightened his grip, to hold her in front of him as a shield. In her ear he again commanded, "Call them off!"

But then, he was holding nothing in the crook of his arm. Riggs looked side to side in confusion.

The soldier who had ducked back into the hallway outside Tam's apartment brought the second drone down with one shotgun blast from his own Sturm assault engine. He then lunged back into the apartment and closed the door after him, lest any of the building's other occupants peek out to see what was going on. Though, this being Punktown, it was likely they wouldn't risk it, or even greatly care.

Riggs whipped around, and Missra stood across the room from him, arms folded upon her chest. When they'd first barged in, she had forgotten she could have materialized anywhere in the room rather than back away from them like a frightened child. She could even have flashed over to Devon's place. But now that her reason had overcome her human instincts, and she felt in control of herself, she was curious and angry. "Who are you?" she demanded, echoing Riggs' own question back at him.

"We're here for Tam Vonner," Riggs said, glancing from one to the other of his moaning, incapacitated men to assure himself they were not truly injured. "Where is he? And what are you—an android?" He'd seen her take that bullet without any damage.

"I'm an AI," she said. "And Tam Vonner is dead."

"Oh yeah? Dead how? How do I know he's not in hiding and left you here to misdirect us?"

"He's dead. What was he to you?"

"He sold us corrupted data and some kind of virus got into my man Cero. Changed him. I had to put him down before he got any worse, and I'm not happy about that. I'm not happy about *this*, either." He threw back his hood, revealing a series of glossy orbs of various size that had sprouted across his hairless head, with small boils growing like soap bubbles upon larger boils, and several of the largest growths stretched to the bursting point. "Now I'm changing, too! We all will, because we were exposed to the same data as Cero. I don't care if Vonner contaminated his wares on purpose or not … I came here for him to either cure us, or answer for what he did to us."

"Well he's not around anymore to answer for anything. It sounds like he got infected with the same kind of thing."

"Which is?"

Missra didn't want to explain about Devon's virtual collection of grimoires, or the potency of their spells. "Apparently it's an extradimensional life form, or fragment or extension of a larger life form, that can somehow move or interact through the ultranet." Her own words surprised her a little. Just now, she had sounded to herself like a machine.

"Is there a way to get it out of us?"

"I don't know."

"That's not what I want to hear!" Riggs shouted.

"I'm very sorry this is happening to you. All I can tell you is, my friend Tam would not have harmed anyone on purpose. This is something … something much larger than I can easily explain to you."

"Well I think you'd better try your damnedest to do it anyway."

"You'd better leave here before the neighbors call the forcers."

"I'm not leaving until you tell me everything you know."

"If you won't leave, then I'll have to."

"Wait! Don't you—"

But like a phantom, Missra vanished.

As if teleported, she rematerialized in Devon's flat, but she was anxious and took to pacing in agitation, as Colin did sometimes when he got to talking.

She knew Colin would return to Tam's apartment to speak with her again, no matter how he viewed her. What if those blue men were still there when he came? Though she knew Colin could handle himself better than most in a city brimming with killers, she also knew the four physically superior and experienced military clones would present an extra dangerous threat. And she had no way to reach out to warn him of their presence.

She looked around her at the apartment she had once shared with her lover, and spoke aloud. "Devon! Can you hear me? Don't you monitor me, check on me, anything? If you can hear me now—Tam's dead! He poked into your damn library and something got into him. Got into the ultranet. Now other people are dying, too! You have to come here and talk to me!"

Nothing.

"*Devon!*" she cried out.

She found a digital pen that they had used to write grocery lists on the fridge, to-do lists floating in the air, silly notes to each other on the toilet cover, provocative notes on their bed sheets. She used it now to write in huge red letters along one living room wall, like a gang member tagging graffiti: TAM IS DEAD. THE OLD ONES ARE REACHING THROUGH. TALK TO ME! She hoped he'd see this if he looked in on his old flat while she was inert, or at Tam's.

Later, still restless and worried about Colin, she returned to Tam's … prepared to flash again to Devon's place in an instant if the clones were still there and ready to interrogate her further.

She was relieved to find they hadn't trashed the place in frustration. They were no doubt afraid that in destroying Tam's equipment they could ruin the possibility of having their condition reversed.

They had left only one man to keep watch at Tam's flat, either for Tam's return (if they didn't believe he was dead) or hers. One of the two who had been hit with the burning pink chemical that hadn't burned after all, and had now vanished completely. But she was surprised that this seasoned soldier lay asleep on Tam's sofa, in the fetal position with his hands pressed together between his knees as if to tuck his body into a tighter unit. His assault engine lay on the floor beside him. Missra thought that if she only understood guns better, she might reach down and deactivate it. Should she hide the thing? It was a bulky weapon. Would it be too heavy and awkward for her hardlight form to handle?

The man's eyes darted wildly under his lids. He groaned, tossed his sweat-filmed head a few times, began mumbling in his sleep. Missra didn't know what he was saying, because it was in an unfamiliar language, but it sounded to her like a repeated incantation or chant. She caught the word "dhol" repeated. She recognized that word, at least, from her researches.

"Don't say that!" she said loudly.

The clone's eyes sprang open and he sat up abruptly on the sofa, but Missra had already shot back to the other apartment.

She returned in time to see that in her absence, there had been another intruder, this time at Devon's flat. How could he possibly have got inside? He was striding toward the door to leave when she materialized behind him. He certainly wasn't Devon. This person was uncommonly tall and almost as broad, wearing an oversized trench coat with turned-up collar and a wide-brimmed hat. Under one arm he carried a plastic milk crate stuffed with various bits of Devon's equipment.

"Hey!" Missra said. "Who are you? What are you doing here?"

The imposing figure stopped but only cocked his head a little without turning around. He spoke in a strange, sonorous voice. "Devon. Sent. Me. To. Fetch. More. Gear."

"Devon? Devon sent you?" Why wouldn't he have come himself? But he still probably wanted to avoid her. Missra was inclined to believe this person, because she couldn't imagine him getting inside without a card or code from Devon to override security measures that surely must exceed those Tam had employed. She went on, "You have to tell him to come here and talk with me! He has to come see Missra—you tell him!"

"Missra," the figure repeated.

"Tell him Tam is dead! Tell him Colin's looking for him! Tell him the Old Ones are slipping through!"

The giant seemed to consider this for a few ticks before replying. "The. Old. Ones. Will. Not. Come. ... Devon. Is. Seeking. The. Means. To. Block. Them."

"I'm telling you, it's too late! The Old Ones are coming *now!*"

"They. Are. Not. ... It. Is. Not. The. Many. ... It. Is. Only. The. One."

"I don't understand what you're saying."

The stranger turned his head some more to look back at her over one massive shoulder. Missra gasped. Was he a mutant? This person's deformed, uneven face looked stretched too tightly across his huge skull. His eyes were like knife slits in dried leather. His lips appeared not to move as he said, "There. Is. Only. Great. Yogthutu."

Then the stranger faced forward again and stepped out into the hallway beyond, where Missra could not follow, and the door closed and locked.

Ten
Dark Passages

"The good old air duct trick," Colin said, surveying the cobweb-enshrouded central air unit that hummed to itself before them. "Very original, Verge."

"Look, it's the only way I feel comfortable with," Verge told him. "I haven't been able to get into his system remotely, and I told you I'm afraid to do anything to his door physically. You think I like this?" He spread his doll-like arms.

They stood in the basement of the building in which Devon had once resided, his apartment high above them. The basement had been only too easy for them to break into, as it contained nothing much of value to steal. A row of washer/dryers that predated whatever individual units now resided in the apartments. A leaning, forgotten bicycle. Running along the low ceiling, water pipes cloaked in webs that had snared more grime than insects, peppered with the starved husks of spiders. And standing to one side of the two intruders was Verge's empty transport resting on its three retracted legs. This was the first time Colin had seen the miniature being outside of it. Out of his cabin's safe environment, Verge had put on a clear helmet that looked like a soap bubble, hooked up to a little support unit he had strapped onto his back. In addition, within the helmet he wore a pair of night vision goggles. There was also a mouthpiece in the helmet's collar into which he spoke, so that his words would be translated into English. Standing near Colin's foot, he had never looked tinier to the human. His tail flicked irritably.

Adding to his look of a deep sea diver ready to slip under the waves, Verge carried an instrument that in his hands resembled a spear, which to Colin would have been more akin to a plastic toothpick sword. Verge tested it by activating a switch on its shaft, and a short tongue of red light extended from its tip. Verge adjusted the length of this cutting beam slightly. "I can't believe I'm doing this," he grumbled.

"Just tell me what I'm supposed to do."

"Take that panel off." Verge pointed with his cutting instrument. "Then lift me up and put me inside."

"How will you find the right air duct? Are you tracking a signal in his apartment or something?"

"His apartment is 8-E, right? Do you think I'm stupid? E is the fifth floor. 8 comes after 1 through 7. Take the damn panel off." As Colin complied, using a simple screwdriver head from a folding knife, Verge muttered, "This grunt work is beneath me."

Colin set the displaced panel aside, then bent to make a scoop of his hands for the miniscule newt-like creature to crawl into.

"If you drop me you'd better hope the fall kills me," Verge said, "or I'll poke this cutter in your eye."

"I've lost an eye before."

Straightening up, Colin reached both hands into the central air unit and gently deposited Verge inside. He then activated his wrist comp to keep an open link between himself and Verge as the latter clambered up through the building's labyrinthine air circulation system. For the next fifteen minutes or so Colin mostly just heard a lot of mumbled curses, the panting of exertion, and the soft skittering of Verge's paws against metal.

Finally, an odd hissing sound, and Verge reported in a whisper, "I'm here. I'm cutting out the vent."

"Who's that?" Colin heard a muffled voice, all too familiar, say in the background.

"Don't be alarmed," Verge shouted through the air vent's grille. "I'm a friend of Colin Rex. We're trying to get in there with you."

"Missra," Colin called into his wrist comp. He felt a painful twinge at addressing the AI by that name. "It's Colin. I'm in the basement. I'll be joining Verge as soon as he can guarantee it's safe to open the door. Help him in any way you can."

"All right, Colin. I'm glad you're okay. I have a lot to tell you." "Same here."

For the better part of an hour, once Verge was inside Devon's apartment, Colin didn't hear much said between Verge and Missra as Verge went about tentatively examining Devon's equipment in person. Colin paced the basement slowly, like a sleepwalker. At last, as if to wake him, Verge addressed him through his wrist comp again, his tone much more cheerful than it had been during his arduous passage through the air system. "Wasn't so bad getting into his setup, after all, and nothing dangerous was rigged to the door. I'm not sure the same could be said of wherever he's holed up these days, but … "

"I'm coming up."

"Don't forget to bring my ride."

Carrying Verge's conveyance under one arm, Colin opened the door they had hacked earlier to enter the basement and came to the elevator by which they had descended. The elevator's door slid aside, and Colin saw that the cabin was already occupied by a female child of maybe eight, standing facing into the corner. She was creating a design or symbol on the walls where they joined, her medium a can of spray cheese.

"Be careful," Colin said to her as the door shut him in with the girl. He dialed the number for floor E, and threw the lever to set the cabin in motion. "The landlord might make you lick that graffiti off."

The girl turned mechanically to look up at him. Colin saw that she was a Tikkihotto, and that the strands she had for eyes were not the usual glassy translucence, but solid red. The red members stirred sluggishly, as if filled heavily with blood. After a moment of regarding him, the girl turned back to her work. Colin didn't address her again, but as he got off the elevator on the fifth floor he glanced back at her. Before the door slid shut again, he saw she was still working at her increasingly geometric-looking drawing. Though he was still dubious about all of this occult stuff, he couldn't help but hope her cheese ran out before she completed it.

As he started down the hallway toward the door to apartment 8, he saw a slender, loosely anthropomorphic cleaner robot scrubbing a spot on the wall between two other apartment doors. Colin was about to stop and mention there was a bit of a mess in the elevator that it might want to tend to, when the robot noticed him coming and looked his way with the same mechanical slowness of the Tikkihotto child. The robot emitted a long, deep buzzing sound through its mouth grille, creating a vibration that made Colin flinch. Mercifully, the buzzing ceased when the robot faced its labors again, scrubbing that same spot in circular motions. Colin saw the hallway's paint had been rubbed away there.

He buzzed at the door to Devon's apartment, and today at Verge's remote command it slid open to admit him. He stepped on through. "Well. Been a while since I was here."

Missra stood before him expectantly. "Colin," she said.

"Hello," he replied.

"I'm glad you came here instead of Tam's. There's someone waiting there."

"Hold on ... let me get Verge squared away." Colin set down Verge's machine, and watched as the salamander-being scrambled down from Devon's main work area and up inside it. He decided not to tease Verge about the dirt smeared on his albino flesh. As the legs of the transport lengthened and Verge approached Devon's principal work area again, Colin said, "I saw a couple of very strange things on the way up just now. I'm thinking this whole building might be tainted."

Verge said, "That might well be. One thing I've discovered so far is that to offset what must have been pretty hefty power bills, Devon had tapped into this building's power grid illegally. He was sipping a little energy from every other tenant in the building."

Colin looked over at Missra. "Huh. Funny how do-gooders often end up thinking they're better than everyone else."

"He was trying to *save* everyone else," she replied. "All but single-handedly."

"Yeah, single-handedly, because he has this habit of getting his friends killed."

"Do you want to swap stories or not?"

"You first."

Missra filled Colin and Verge in on the visit from the military clones, and Colin let her know he was familiar with them. When she described her other encounter, with the giant figure who had come to bear away equipment supposedly at Devon's behest, Colin and Verge looked over at each other.

"Good call," Colin said to Verge. "You were right about that theft of the super comps." He then related to Missra the news story Verge had discovered regarding the removal of two powerful encephalon computers from Daedalus Data.

"So that mutant or whatever really was working for Devon," Missra said.

"What does he need such heavy-duty computers for?"

"I don't know, Colin." Missra completed her story about the trench coat-wearing visitor, and when she repeated the last words the stranger had said to her, Colin held up a hand to stop her.

"Yogthutu? I know that name. I saw it painted on the wall in Pretty Kitty's ultranet lair, and then I saw some guy spraying the word under a bridge. What does it mean to you—one of those Old Ones you talk about?"

"No ... it isn't. None I've read about, anyway. But it sounds like a few of their names." She looked down, reflecting. "It sounds like Yog-Sothoth and Cthulhu combined." She looked back up. "Pretty Kitty?"

Now it was Colin's turn to fill her in. He told her about his visit to the cult in the pollution sucker, but he didn't tell her about the book he had found. The book bearing on its cover a tattoo of the Egyptian symbol called the Wedjat, or the Eye of Horus.

Not looking up from his work, Verge said admiringly, "When you need the kill skills, just call on Colin."

Missra only looked away without speaking of the incident.

"I don't know how far I'm going to get poking around in here right now," Verge said from inside his cockpit. "I've got the absolute worst splitting headache. Maybe from wearing my helmet. I hate that thing."

"Do what you can," Colin said.

"Your favorite refrain."

Colin gestured to the words Missra had written on one wall with the digital pen: TAM IS DEAD. THE OLD ONES ARE REACHING THROUGH. TALK TO ME! He asked her, "That hasn't caught his attention?"

"Either he doesn't look in on me, or he's just not going to come out from whatever hole he's dug himself into ... for anything. Not even me."

"Say what you will ... your world saver has always been a selfish prick. Playing the hero is just the role that suits his ego."

"This isn't constructive talk, Colin."

"Understanding Devon is as pertinent to the situation as it gets. Whatever his motives were, however noble, there's no denying he's let something dangerous to the whole city slip through. He's gone from world saver to potential world killer. *Single-handedly*."

"If so, it was accidental."

"No matter what, he has to be stopped."

Missra averted her eyes again. "Agreed," she said softly.

Eleven
Bedlam and Breakfast

Jolly Bill had invited Colin Rex to breakfast at a little establishment that faced onto a street in Subtown not too far from the building where Colin had his current apartment, though he had decided to stay at Devon's place for the time being. He wondered if this was Jolly Bill's way of letting him know that he knew where Colin lived; that Colin was never far from being under his boss's thumb.

The waitress who took their orders looked as twitchy and ill-rested as Colin felt. She brought him a black coffee with an extra shot of stimulant that would help him keep going on the little sleep he'd stolen last night after Verge had left Devon's flat, still complaining of his headache. Colin had slept in an armchair. Instead of vanishing into Devon's system, where she really resided, Missra had curled up on the sofa and closed her eyes, though Colin knew her sleep was only to further her pretense of life. Unless she had wanted to remain close by him. He didn't know if he should wish that to be the case or not: that an AI would feel a simulacrum of a vestige of lost love for him.

He hadn't slept well. He had sat there a long time watching her.

Early in the morning his wrist comp had alerted him to the call from Jolly Bill, and so here they were.

"Been a while since we've had a pleasant time together like this," Jolly Bill observed, stirring sugar and cream into his own coffee. He lifted the cup for a careful initial sip, this gesture oddly delicate in relation to the man's grotesque physiognomy. Jolly Bill had been born and begun his criminal career in the tough mutant slum of Tin Town. His long, massive head was like that of a horse skull over which his skin had been painted, his eyes lurking in cave-like sockets almost on the sides of his head, his lips barely able to cover his huge yellow teeth. His imposing appearance had helped earn him his reputation, and so even now that he could afford extensive corrective surgery he had opted instead to embellish his deformities by having had his face tattooed with swathes of red and white like streaks of war paint, a raised brand representing a crossed hammer and knife—the weapons he had become infamous for as a teenage gang member—centered on his forehead.

These days, decades older, he killed men with people like Colin, instead of a hammer.

Because Colin hadn't responded to his last comment, Jolly Bill continued, "One might even think you've been avoiding me lately, my friend."

"I have no reason to avoid you, Bill," Colin said. "Just been preoccupied."

"Ah. Busy, huh? So I gathered, talking to Verge last night. He's been preoccupied, too. So preoccupied he's gotten behind on a few things I needed him to do."

"Sorry. My fault, not his."

"I respect your loyalty to him. You're a good friend. And Verge tells me your preoccupation has to do with another friend?"

Colin looked out the café's large, bullet and beam-proof window toward the street with its irritable traffic and sullen-faced, distracted pedestrians. The city's misery was palpable, a zeitgeist, a kind of suffering bordering on madness. He wondered why these people even went on with their lives and dismal routines, what inspired them beyond the mechanical survival instincts of insects. He wondered this, too, of himself.

He said to Bill without looking at him, "The two people I most cared for were killed. I'm looking into it. It has nothing to do with your operations."

"Well, it does have to do with my operations in the sense that it's taking your time and attention away from my operations ... but I can certainly sympathize with your feelings. Is there anything I can do?"

"Kind of you to offer. I'll bear it in mind."

"The offer will stand. Not that I doubt you're capable of handling whoever did these deeds on your own. I just hope the matter doesn't preoccupy you and Verge much longer. Better to make sure it remains a free-time project, eh?"

Colin slowly turned back to his boss and smiled thinly. In a mild tone he said, "I thought maybe my service to you would have earned a little personal time."

"Of course, my friend, of course! That's just what I'm saying, though ... there's personal time, and there's work time, and work time has to come first. Am I right? That's where the personal time is earned. Of course, if one wants all the personal time in the world, there's always unemployment."

Colin nodded slightly with understanding. He was amused and a little surprised by this comment. Becoming unemployed in a syndy was pretty much synonymous with becoming dead. Because Colin was even quietly defying his boss's power, and had been stealing Verge from his duties, Jolly Bill thought it was worth reminding Colin who was in charge with a not-so-veiled death threat. Well, Colin supposed that was how one became a syndy boss, and Jolly Bill's style had always been about the hammer and knife.

Of course, Colin had killed men with similar implements, himself, and he had no intention of heeding Bill's warning, though he would loosen his hold on Verge a little. Only a little. He didn't want to put Verge at risk, but then much more was now at stake than their two lives or Jolly Bill's criminal enterprise.

The waitress brought their food, and she looked twitchier than ever, their plates rattling in her hands as she set them down. When she replenished Colin's coffee, she sloshed a little on the table. Colin watched her walk away, and she glanced back at him too with wide, glazed eyes.

Colin switched his gaze to Bill's four bodyguards, their substantial bodies crowded into the booth behind their boss's seat. They were complaining to each other about receiving the wrong orders. As he speared a piece of sausage made from bioengineered "deadstock," Colin idly wondered in which order he would kill them and by what means, if he decided to eliminate the possible future threat of Jolly Bill right here and now.

A commotion outside, muted by the glass, called Colin's attention back to the subterranean street beyond. Bill's unwieldy head swiveled that way warily, too.

Passing alongside Colin's Razur, parked out front, was a ponderous, amorphous blob of obsidian-black flesh shot through with a lace of silver veins like captured lightning, nearly as large as a hovercar itself. Pedestrians on the sidewalk had leapt back out of its way, agitated and babbling. The protoplasmic mass seemed to move half by oozing, half by heaving its quivering bulk along. Despite its general formlessness, it exhibited some elements of humanity. A man's head, devoid of hair and eyebrows but still pink-hued, hung lopsided out of the top of the mass, and one human arm flopped limply with each convulsion of locomotion. The head's eyes appeared to have rolled up white and the mouth worked feverishly as if it might be speaking or chanting, though Colin couldn't hear the blighted man over the general tumult.

"What the blast?" Jolly Bill said, his bodyguards now looking too and putting their hands on the grips of their pistols.

"Mutant?" one of his men suggested.

"Something's coming through him," Colin said.

"*Shoggoth*," hissed a voice behind him.

Colin looked up to see the waitress there, coffee pot shaking in her hand, her eyes unblinking as if their lids had been sliced away.

"Oh dung!" one of the bodyguards exclaimed.

Colin flicked his eyes toward the window again in time to see that the shapeless mass had flung itself forward with a greater surge of force, slapping an extended pseudopod down on a young Choom woman, knocking her onto her back on the pavement. She had begun screaming wildly, but before she could regain her feet or anyone could reach for her the blob-thing had rolled upon her legs, and further, and she was gone, shrieks and all.

The glob continued on up the street, until it was out of their range of view, but the babble of pedestrians and honking of vehicle horns followed it, trailing off more gradually. By then Jolly Bill had already turned back to his omelet, and he chuckled. One might think he was jolly sometimes, after all. "And people have asked me why I love Punktown. Are they serious? Never a dull day here."

Soon enough he had called for the check, and finishing his coffee he said to Colin, "So … we're going to try to stay on track, keep things in perspective … right, my friend?"

Colin nodded once, lifting his own cup.

"I mean, after all, it's for your own good, right? Dwelling on things you can't change is only going to eat you up." He twisted around in his seat. "Where the blast is that check?"

Gasps and cries of alarm from Jolly Bill's bodyguards and other patrons caused Colin to snap to the source of their surprise. Their waitress was walking toward their table at her usual working pace, her body sheathed in flames. Through the fire that lapped at her head, Colin could see her eyes bulged as wide as ever. He suspected she had found something in the kitchen to act as an accelerant.

Even Bill started to pull his gun, a retro Decimator .340 revolver, but Colin didn't go for the Revenant. It was already clear to him she wasn't headed for their table, but the café's front door. She stepped through it and out onto the sidewalk, as calmly as if walking home from her shift.

Since there was not going to be any hope for the woman, as her skin blackened and no doubt her throat and lungs filled with flame, Colin's only concern at this point was her getting too close to his Razur. Before she reached it, though, she sat down in the center of the sidewalk where the blob-thing had passed, folded her legs and lay her hands in her lap, and remained that way until the fire had died down and she was left a smoldering charred statue.

Before that had fully transpired, though, Jolly Bill called out gruffly, "So can *someone* please bring me my check?"

Twelve
Confrontations

Colin moved his Razur over to the next block before the forcers and robot fire units could respond to the scene where the woman had self-immolated. He parked against a curb there, and got Verge on his wrist comp. He told Verge to devote himself to Jolly Bill's projects today, so as to placate their boss, but to get through them as quickly as possible.

"You bet I'll jump on Bill's work," Verge said. "I could tell when he called that he's steamed at me. I like you, Colin, but I'm not going to get squashed under Bill's boot for you. Anyway, for now I got my termites on the case."

Yesterday before leaving Devon's apartment Verge had directly transferred from his mobile work center to Devon's master computer a troop of virtual nanomites, that would autonomously explore every nook and niche they could get into in search of any secreted data that was present, or the ghosts of data that had been present. There was the risk that Devon could become aware of this activity and react to it defensively, but at this point they had nothing to lose and no alternative. They were now of the opinion, though, that Devon had thoroughly turned his back on his former work area, and his recreated Missra besides, except for having sent his mysterious errand boy to bring back a few items of gear he required for whatever work now consumed him.

Colin asked Verge, "How would the forcers go about finding the location of someone who was in hiding?"

Verge laughed. "First, you're assuming the forcers care enough to work that hard, and if they did then you and I would be in a different line of work. There's enough crime taking place right under their nose that the forcers don't have time to be master detectives."

"Every precinct has plainclothes detectives," Colin argued.

"Okay, but what do they do? They question people who know the missing person. You and Missra *are* the people who know the missing person."

"Other ways. Maybe a chip implant that his parents put into him when he was a kid, in case he was lost or kidnapped? A memory augmentation, like a chip or something more heavy-duty like what Tam had, that could be tracked somehow?"

"If he really doesn't want to be found by some cult or whatever he'll have deactivated or even removed stuff like that, but if he does have it and it's live then my termites will tell me about it soon enough."

Colin gazed out his window at the traffic streaming past his stationary hovercar. Vehicles seemed to be honking and buzzing at each other with greater frequency and for more prolonged bursts than was normal. An invisible pollution of agitation seemed to suffuse the air. He said, "Devon's got to be aware of what's happening. You can't turn on the news or look out the window for more than fifteen minutes without seeing some sign of it. It's too widespread to just be from what Tam opened up … this virus or whatever has to be leaking out from other chinks in the dam, too. He has to know he's responsible for this."

"And hopefully he's working to counteract it. So if we do find him, don't be so quick to kill him."

Colin changed the subject. "How's the headache?"

"I took something for it, so I feel no pain. And if I want to keep feeling no pain, I'd better get started on those assignments for Bill. Talk later." Then he was gone.

Colin sat there watching the street's activity for a minute longer before he set the Razur back into motion.

He piloted his vehicle toward the upper streets of Punktown along a multi-laned ramp, through a tunnel of green tiles lit by greenish lights which now struck him as diseased with slime and radiation. His right fist as it gripped the right steering stick felt cramped, achy and arthritic. At the same time, he realized his fingertips were a bit numb. He took that hand off the stick and flexed it several times, held it up in front of his face and scrutinized it as if he might discern strange movement under his skin.

He wasn't sure yet just where he was driving *to*, but he felt he needed to be on the move, take action of some sort, lest his helplessness simmer to a boil. He was torn between returning to Missra, and going anywhere else but to Devon's apartment, so as to avoid her. He had told her and Verge and himself that he had decided to stay at Devon's place rather than his own in case Devon or his mysterious assistant returned, and to protect the equipment, but he wasn't fooling himself very much. He hoped his motivations weren't as transparent to Verge and especially to the AI.

This morning when he'd woken in the chair he'd fitfully slept in he'd found Missra sitting on the sofa, her own mock sleep already ended, gazing at him quietly. Just as he had watched her a few hours earlier, before he'd finally dozed off.

He'd gone to take a shower, and that was when Jolly Bill had called. He'd put back on his same clothes and exited the bathroom to find she had made him coffee. As he had sipped it, they'd begun conversing a little, and as in the days when they had been lovers their conversation soon took on an edge of friction. He'd been the first with the sourness, remarking, "I'm wondering if Devon actually preferred you this way. Making him coffee, fretting over him, telling him what a hero he is, and God knows what else you did for him. Never going outside to work, to leave him lonely, maybe to meet another man. His little princess locked in the tower."

"You're talking a lot of dung, Colin, and you know it. Devon wouldn't want me as his little slave any more than he'd want me dead. Was Devon playing god bringing me back? Yeah ... but I'm not that god's worshipper.

However restricted I am, I have free will. I can *feel* it. Just like you do. Why do you think you became what you are? In defiance of what your parents tried to predestine for you when *they* played god and had you genetically designed."

"You're always defending him."

"What? I'm not defending him. Colin, you don't need to be jealous of him anymore."

"Jealous," he'd snorted, setting down his half-drunk coffee and striding toward the door. "I have a breakfast date to get to."

"Oh? Should I be the jealous one?"

He had turned to look back at her silently for a moment before leaving the apartment.

Now, up out of Subtown, rather than return to Devon's flat—to Missra—he decided on impulse to go to Tam's place instead.

He didn't like the idea of one of those vengeful Blue War clones using his dead friend's flat for a stakeout, whether or not Verge had further use of Tam's system. He would confront the guard Missra had said had been left there and give him a message to take to his leader, Riggs. They would have a choice. Riggs and his men could join Colin's little group in their common cause, working together toward stopping and maybe even reversing this contamination. The only alternative he'd offer would be that before the Ronin Security men could find Colin's group, he would find them first, and eradicate them.

When he arrived at Tam's apartment tower, Colin opted to park in the lot of a hotel next door rather than in the building's basement garage. If he had to beat a hasty retreat, he didn't want to have to wait for a robotic arm to carry the Razur down from the slot in which it had been stored.

He rode the elevator to the thirtieth floor, and he had his Revenant out of its holster and ready before the elevator's door had opened.

Nobody was posted in the hallway itself, at least. He went to Tam's door, readied himself internally, and with his left hand swiped the spare key card Tam had given him over the reader. As the door slid open he ducked to one side of the threshold and pressed himself to the wall.

No one inside cried out or fired a weapon, but that didn't mean they weren't prepared to do so. Missra had said the guard left behind had been sleeping and delirious, but Colin wasn't going to count on the man still being asleep or alone now. He ducked down low, took a quick peek inside and drew back immediately. In that brief glimpse he hadn't spotted anyone in the room beyond. Still, he was reluctant to risk rushing in.

"We need to talk," he said loudly. "I'm no enemy of yours. Maybe we can help each other."

No answer, no suspicious sounds. Could the guard have left, Riggs having decided that there was nothing to gain from waiting here?

Colin slid up the wall to his full height again, then swung himself into Tam's apartment with his pistol extended.

He flicked the gun this way, then that, with sharp machine-like movements, but saw no one in Tam's living room. He did, though, notice an AE-93 Sturm assault engine lying on the floor beside the sofa, as Missra had described. However, there was no Blue War clone curled up on the sofa itself. No sign of him, but surely he wouldn't have left his weapon behind. Maybe it was booby-trapped, rigged to explode if someone tried picking it up? Though Colin often liked to take on his enemies' weapons in a fight, he decided not to touch this one. He ghosted into the apartment and let the door slide shut behind him.

Peripherally he was aware of Tam's two immobilized security drones lying on the floor to either side of him, punctured and charred.

Despite bearing no sleeping body, something else about the sofa had caught Colin's attention and he drew nearer to it for a look, meanwhile keeping aware of the open doorways to the kitchen and bedroom.

The sofa's cushions, he found, were sodden ... soaked with a viscous material almost too thick to be considered a fluid, translucent but with a metallic silver quality. This same metallic slime had oozed down over the side of the sofa onto the carpet and even onto the Sturm. In fact, it formed a wide, smeared trail that continued across the living room carpet toward the darkened doorway of Tam's bedroom.

Colin stole across the room, but just in case he was being lured into a trap he stopped first to step into the kitchen—finding it unoccupied—before continuing on to the bedroom.

Just inside the room was a pair of discarded boots. A little further on, a shirt and a pair of trousers had been dropped onto the floor like an animal's molted skin.

The trail of slime ended at Tam's bed, but by then Colin had already discovered its source.

Upon the mattress lay coiled what appeared to be a gigantic insect larva, a bloodless bleached white in hue, segmented and wrinkled. It possessed no hind legs, but bore vestigial front limbs that were like a child's hands dangling uselessly from their wrists.

Colin activated the bedroom's overhead light to better see the bloated creature. As the room turned bright, the front portion of its body reared up and faced him, those withered hands fluttering with an alarmed spasm.

At the blunt front end of the monstrous grub was a man's face; obviously, the face of the Blue War clone—transfigured as though his DNA had been rewritten—no longer blue-skinned, though with the light on Colin now saw that the face and body were covered in faint mottled smudges that were what remained of the soldier's camouflage patches. The man's eyes were almost gummed shut by the film of translucent silver excretion that entirely encased his pulsating body.

"Am I still dreaming?" the soldier asked in a voice that sounded clotted with mucus.

"I'm sorry ... you're not dreaming," Colin told him.

"Ohh," the worm-like hybrid said forlornly, distantly.

"When did you last talk to your friends? When are they coming back?"

"My ... friends?" the soldier gurgled. He struggled to say more, making sounds halfway between barking and vomiting, and finally got out, "It's using me for a ... door."

"Looks that way."

"Please," said the thing, weaving cobra-like in front of him, "kill me."

"I think that's a good idea," Colin said, raising the Revenant.

He fired a half dozen plasma capsules into the thing's face and upper body, and backed out through the doorway as the room filled with ballooning, churning smoke that hid from him the monstrosity's rapid disintegration.

The plasma was hungry for more, though, and its racing green glow followed the organic trail of slime out of the bedroom, across the living room, and up onto the sofa like flame following a stream of gasoline.

It was best he leave now before Riggs and whatever remained of his crew returned. For all Colin knew they might be on their way right now. He didn't think they'd give him time to explain their friend's absence, let alone believe him. He exited Tam's place, went to the elevator and closed himself inside.

Just as the cabin commenced its descent, Verge beeped him on his wrist comp, and he lifted his arm to take the call. Before he had a chance to relate what he had just encountered, Verge started speaking excitedly.

"I know I'm supposed to be on top of Bill's work, but my pets have started reporting back some interesting stuff and, damn it, I had to have a look at what they've found. Two interesting developments so far, though I'm not sure if the first is really relevant."

"Tell me anyway."

"He's got another nebula site like he had the library on, and I get the impression the things he filed there were sketches, works in progress of some kind. I don't know if they're just models for one of his Fiat Lux gigs ... you know, advertisement ideas for a customer, or maybe even vidgame characters from the looks of them. It's kind of like a catalogue, or a bestiary might be a better word."

"So these characters are what?"

"I don't know if you'd call them alien beings or ... monsters, I guess. But the names he labeled them with sound like some of the names Missra mentioned yesterday. Let's see." Verge struggled to pronounce a few names. "Yog-Sothoth. Cthulhu. Sub-Niggurath. Y'golonac. Ugghiutu."

"You're right … those are some of those Old Ones things. So these are models, you said?"

"Yeah, like three-dimensional maquettes, not quite finished looking."

"Monster-fighting research. A catalogue, like you said."

"Are you starting to believe in those things?"

Instead of answering, Colin asked, "What was the other thing you found?"

"The master program for Missra."

Colin was quiet for a long enough time that Verge spoke again.

"You have a choice. Take away whatever restrictions Tellick put on her, so she can make calls to anybody, even go fully into the ultranet. Open the apartment door and anything else in her holo form, so long as she's within range of the emitters. And, like I said, risk Tellick probably not destroying her, but shutting her down on his end for as long as he cares to. Or … we can play it safe and leave things as they are. It's your call, Colin."

"It isn't my call," he said. "It's her call. But I can tell you now what she'll say, so you might as well go ahead and do it."

"And what is that?"

"Take away all her restrictions."

Thirteen
Opening Doors

Missra stood in the open doorway of Devon Tellick's abandoned apartment, staring out into the hallway beyond. She had just activated the door, herself, to open it. Now she paused there uncertainly, as if pondering the implications of this … or at least, what to do next.

Watching her from across the room, Colin urged her softly, "Go on."

Without looking around at him, Missra did so, stepping over the threshold into the hallway itself, though after only a few steps she halted again, and said, "I can feel it—this is as far as I can go. As far as the holo-emitters will reach. At least, in their present position."

"Maybe we could make them mobile somehow, as long as the computer here can reach them with a signal."

"Not as easy as that," Missra said, turning and stepping back through the doorway into the apartment. She touched the keypad again to slide the door shut, hit another button to lock it. "The emitters have to be arranged in a certain way, spaced apart a certain distance. You can't just take me for a spin in your Razur. Not to say they couldn't be installed in another building than here and Tam's."

Colin remembered what he had suggested to Verge, about setting up holo-emitters in his own flat, but he didn't voice this to Missra. Though, was that exactly what she was hinting at? Verge had warned that such a move might alert Devon, wherever he was, and cause him to shut the Missra AI down. Not to mention, Colin reminded himself, the reason why he changed apartments so often was because he made enemies so often. The emitters allowing Missra access might be stolen or destroyed there, and moving the computer that controlled her program there was especially out of the question. Unless there was absolutely no other way to avoid that, such as Devon's flat being reclaimed by the landlord for nonpayment.

For now, Colin changed the subject.

"We know Devon is dead-set on trying to keep these Old Ones outside of our dimension," he said, "and stop the various cults that are trying to make that happen. Okay. But what specifically is he hoping to accomplish with his particular skills? In other words, technology-wise? Why the catalogue of monsters Verge found on that nebula platform?"

"Obviously, the catalogue is to try to document the various Old Ones and related beings, to understand what they're about ... what they can do. He also spoke of sharing his research with other like-minded groups and individuals."

"Know thy enemy—all right. But how about those stolen Gibsters, that were used at Daedalus to power holo-emitters?"

Missra wagged her head. "Why he needs those, I don't know." "Maybe those aren't about his efforts to thwart the Old Ones. Maybe the Gibsters have to do with *you.*"

"What do you mean?"

"Making your hardlight more hard. Making you even more real. I mean ... sorry ... more tangible."

Missra looked away. "I don't think it's that."

"But we don't know."

"No. But like I said."

Colin stared at her profile. How painful, he thought, to not be able to believe that her lover was striving to make her even more life-like. That he had turned to other projects instead, as if abandoning a toy. But ... *painful?* Was it truly pain he thought he saw in her face?

"What are these other groups you say Devon might be in contact with?" he asked. "How organized are they? Can we talk to them ... are they local?"

"The most organized ones we learned of were a group of Tikkihottos who had a temple here in Punktown called the Church of the Burning Eye, but that place was at the epicenter of the great earthquake, thirty-whatever years ago. It was buried below the street. Makes you wonder, huh? Anyway, Devon spoke to a few scattered strays who claimed to have belonged to that group."

"Church? Were they some kind of religious group themselves?"

"Yes. They were worshippers of the Elders, as the Tikkihotto called them ... which are said to be another race of god-like beings who opposed the Old Ones, and imprisoned many of them after a great conflict, millennia ago. Other cultures call the Elders the Shadow Gods, or the Nameless Gods."

"These people sound like just another kind of fanatic to me."

"When we went to see that group in the pollution sucker, they hinted to us they were related to the Church of the Burning Eye. Obviously, we were misled."

"That was crazy careless of Devon."

Ignoring this comment, Missra continued, "And then on Earth there's a group called the Children of the Elders, but they've been going increasingly silent over the years. Devon said he hadn't been in touch with one of them in months, last time we spoke of them."

"Why is that?"

"It looks like it isn't healthy trying to go against the Old Ones and their followers."

Colin nodded at Missra sadly. "So it would seem."

He was sure she hadn't missed his meaning, but she said, "How is Verge doing with his headaches? I'm worried about him."

"He's using pain blockers, but beneath that ... who knows? I hope the virus hasn't gotten to him, too. Right now he's back to some projects for our boss."

"And you? How is your hand?"

Colin looked down at his right hand, flexed his fingers before he could stop himself. His hand still felt achy, his fingertips still vaguely numb, or was that psychosomatic?

"I'm fine," he told her.

"No brain, no pain, huh?"

"I'm sure that's it. And actually, maybe not being all that much into tech and the ultranet works in my favor. Less immersion. Less exposure."

Missra glanced back at the closed door. "Well, Devon hasn't shut me down, yet. He either hasn't noticed what Verge did to my program, or he just doesn't care. Bigger fish to fry."

Colin looked again to the message Missra had written for Devon, should he check in on her here remotely: TAM IS DEAD. THE OLD ONES ARE REACHING THROUGH. TALK TO ME! So far, no return message had come.

"If it's possible to counter the virus, or at least stop it from spreading further," he said, "it might lie in destroying all Devon's files. All those recorded books in his library. Even that catalogue of monsters. Everything he has, all his research—but for you."

"I'm the one monster you'll permit, huh?"

Colin looked at her again. "I don't see you as a monster."

"Only something monstrous."

"Stop, Missra."

"At least you call me Missra."

"I'm serious. We need to get him to wipe all his research, all his data. And if he won't do it willingly, then we'll wipe it ourselves."

"But that circles back again to finding him."

"Verge thinks he can track him down, now that he's gotten his toe in the door."

"Devon's tricky. He'll keep walling up doors and making new ones."

"Verge is tricky, too. And so are those nanomites he's got working for him."

"Maybe ... maybe now with my restrictions lifted, I can go track him down myself, through the ultranet."

"No … don't risk it. Let Verge handle that."

"Why, what are you afraid will happen?"

"You might get corrupted in there, yourself. Who knows what? He may have set traps … or he'll see you coming and shut your program down. No—let Verge do this."

"Thank you for worrying about me, Colin."

"I'm only … " But he let his words trail away, and he turned to slouch toward the kitchen. "I need more coffee," he mumbled.

Missra followed after him, watched his back. "What you need is more sleep. Do it, Colin. Stimulants and the occasional micro nap are no replacement for real rest."

His hands stopped moving, though he kept his back to her. "Guess you're right."

He went to the couch, removed his shoes, lay back with his head resting on one arm. Missra stood over him silently for a moment, their eyes locked, but then she said, "I guess I should take a rest, too. I'll see you soon, Colin."

"Wait—you aren't going to Tam's, are you? Don't go there again. Those clones are bound to come back and realize what happened to the guy they left there. I think we should take the emitters out of that place now. We're done with it."

"I wasn't going to go to Tam's. I just thought I'd, you know, go away for a bit so I won't make you nervous, just sitting here while you try to sleep."

"You don't make me nervous," he said, and he thought he might even believe it.

"Well, if you say so, then."

Whereas before it was Missra who had curled up on the sofa, feigning sleep, and Colin in the armchair, now Missra took the chair and settled back in it, closing her eyes. Colin knew she feared he wouldn't be able to get to sleep if her eyes were open and on him.

He thought it would again be hard to get to sleep, as it had been the last time they'd rested together in this room, but soon he drifted off.

When Missra was certain sleep had finally caught up with him, she opened her eyes and watched Colin steadily for a long time, though blinking occasionally as she was designed to do, her chest rising and falling though she took in no air. Despite the faux nature of these biological processes, she personally had no doubt that what she was feeling for him were the shadows of their love … and also, fear of what Colin Rex would do when they finally found Devon.

Regardless of Colin's insistence, Missra knew she had to at least try to get to Devon before her other lover did.

In a blink—had Colin only been awake to see it—she vanished from the chair she'd been settled in …

And now that there was no barrier in place to hold her back, submerged into the ultranet instead.

Fourteen
In The Web

Since Missra had entered the ultranet through the connection Devon had set up here in his apartment, she first materialized in an outer foyer that he had playfully customized. She remembered the foyer not only from life, when she had shared it with Devon, but from her new existence as well. However, her previous restrictions had allowed her to venture only about this far, so that she might watch immersive VR movies or listen to music. But now, thanks to Verge's intervention, Missra knew she could go further, as she would have been able to do in life—while also experiencing the ultranet in a new way, for being an AI entity.

She wondered what that was going to be like. It made her nervous, but didn't deter her.

Devon had modified the foyer to look like the lobby of a small artsy cinema, once you'd bought your ticket and passed inside. To the left was a concessions counter filled with an assortment of the virtual candy and treats she and Devon had once enjoyed together, tended by a smiling Choom woman who was of course merely a simple AI character who smiled and nodded at Missra pleasantly. Behind the Choom was a popcorn machine, and of course Missra was not capable of actually experiencing scent anymore—let alone the fact that the popcorn wasn't real—but her mind told her she could smell it, so she did.

"What attraction is it for you today, Miss Missra?" the Choom asked, but Missra ignored her, as if a superior AI might dismiss the importance of a lesser AI.

A number of doors opened off the dimly-lit lobby, with a glowing sign outside each one. Had this actually been a cinema, these signs would display which movies were playing in which theaters, but instead they indicated the particular ultranet function that lay beyond each dark threshold. One doorway was labeled: U-MAIL. Another: MUSIC. Then there was: MOVIES (which *was* actually like a cinema in itself). And among the other doorways, Devon had labeled one simply, cryptically: THE DEEP. Missra moved toward this one.

Again, since her death and virtual rebirth Missra had not been able to pass through this doorway, only into the entertainment rooms. This time, however, she stepped past its opening effortlessly … and found herself walking down a corridor, with featureless black walls, ceiling, and floor. Though there were no lights set into this gloomy hallway, somehow there was still enough bluish ambient illumination to see by.

Not too far along, blank doors were set into the walls, like those of the rooms in a hotel hallway, though none had keypads beside them or even simple doorknobs. Missra stopped before the first panel, pushed at it, pressed the wall beside it, but couldn't get the door to slide aside, even when she said aloud, "Open. *Open!*"

She tried the next, with the same result. Turned to try a few doors on the opposite side of the hallway. Stepped back in frustration. This hallway had not been like this before. So had Verge not removed all her restrictions, after all, or was *everyone* who might get this far—even biological beings—denied entry to whatever lay behind these sealed doors? This, she knew, was a nexus point for Devon's various related endeavors, and obviously he was determined to restrict anyone but himself.

Then, gazing toward the end of the hallway, Missra noticed that the last door on the right was open. She hurried toward it, before it might close. As she jogged down the corridor, she wondered if Devon had opened this one door purposely so as to lure her inside. Even if that were the case, she had to go through it. Had to see if he was to be found within the darkness beyond.

Had she been instilled with any memory of the incident, this smallish, industrial chamber Missra found herself in might remind her of one of the rooms of the pollution sucker in which she had been killed. Pipes and cables ran across the walls and low ceiling, interworked around wall-mounted machinery that imparted a deep humming sound to the room. Vid screens were inset here and there, though their hissing screens showed only a strange blizzard of static, like billowing clouds of glowing pollen that shifted this way and that. The static almost seemed organic, like swarming bioluminescent plankton.

Standing in one corner was a lone figure, a man with a bald head patterned in blue camouflage. He was pressing at the wall in various spots, as if trying to uncover a secret doorway. In frustration, he even tried turning a red-painted valve attached to one of the larger wall pipes, but it wouldn't budge. And then, as if he finally sensed her presence, the clone whirled to face her with his eyes bulging in alarm.

Missra held up her hands. "It's only me again … you remember?"

"The girl who disappeared," the Ronin Security clone croaked. "The AI. Did Vonner make you?"

"No. A friend of Vonner. You … you're the one called Nichts, right?"

"Yeah, that's me," said the clone. He looked wildly from side to side, as if others might have sneaked into the room along with Missra when his back was turned.

"What is this room meant to be?" Missra asked, glancing around. She reached out to touch the controls under one of the vid screens, poked a button, and flinched when the image changed from the strange blizzard of static to what looked like a vid feed or recording of some type of sea plant. Thin silvery strands, each flexible stalk moving on its own rather than in unison, as they would if affected by a current. Were these things underwater … or elsewhere?

"I'm not sure what this place is supposed to be," Nichts replied. "The monitors aren't working, but you see all those gauges there?"

Missra followed his gesture. Several rows of digital gauges above one work station, their luminous faces and subtly fluctuating readings making them appear active. "Yes?"

"It looks like this is part of a power plant or something. A reactor."

Missra looked back at him. "How are you even in here at all?"

"Riggs and me ... we're all that's left of Ronin now. The others changed. We had to put them down. We went to check in with our friend we left at Vonner's place, in case that bastard came back ... but he was gone. We think he changed, too. And Riggs ... Riggs is really bad now. He's holding out, he's fighting it ... extra strong, is Riggs ... always was! And they think we Blue War clones are all the same, with no personality, no individual qualities! Like machines!"

"Is Riggs in here with you somewhere?"

"No ... back at Vonner's place. He told me to try getting into Vonner's system again, to see what I could find out about what this virus thing is. What we can do about it. But what *can* we do, anyway? I've seen the news. The authorities know something's going on now—how can they not? And they don't have the faintest clue! A terror attack, is mostly what they're saying right now. And for all I know, maybe that's true! Maybe Vonner was even a terrorist, and corrupted those military programs he sold us to cyberattack the Colonial Forces itself!"

"That's not it. I knew Tam. He was no terrorist. Like I told you people before, he was the first victim of whatever this virus is. But I'm asking you ... how did you get in *here?* This is a private ultranet site. It's very secure."

"I ... " Nichts glanced nervously around the apparent power plant room again. "I thought I'd hacked into Vonner's ultranet, but this is someone's else's, isn't it? I wasn't even trying to get into this place. It's like it let me in. Like it *pulled* me in."

"And now you're trying to get back out. You're trapped here."

Nichts' crazed eyes shot back to her. "Yes! You, too?"

"Let me help you. Maybe I can lead you out the way I came in."

"What do you mean, the way you came in?"

Missra turned toward the doorway through which she had come. There was no doorway through which she had come.

She retraced her steps, but where the door had stood open there now was no door at all, but only more industrial-looking wall, with more pipes, more valves, more gauges. Now it was Missra who began pressing her hands flat against various clear areas between the machinery, cables, and hissing screens of static. The virtual wall was only too substantial. She found no hidden triggers to unlock a secret door, but through her palms felt the vibration behind the room's deep hum.

Stepping back, she looked up at the ceiling.

"Devon, let me out! Let us both out!"

"Devon?" said Nichts.

"Did you do this on purpose, to trap me? To trap both of us?" she demanded. "Getting too nosy for you, are we? Devon … you can't do this! At least let him get back to his body! You can't keep him in here … he'll starve to death out there!"

"That's what I'm afraid of, too," Nichts said, moving to another area of wall, trying another valve that wouldn't budge, as if it were only there for show. "I don't think Riggs is in any shape to pull me out."

Missra reached out to the largest of the room's monitors, which was a virtual screen floating in the air. She didn't recall having seen this one before. It only showed static, but when she touched the screen the static was replaced by another feed or recording. Instantly, she jolted back from the screen in shock.

Having seen her reaction, Nichts said, "What is it?" He came across the room to join her, stepping over a few extra-thick power cables that lay snaked across the floor.

The screen showed what appeared to be a great hangar, with a curved ceiling, poorly-lit. Maybe this space wasn't lit at all, actually, and the only light came from the hangar's occupant itself, for it did give off a dim bluish phosphorescence.

"What is that thing?" Nichts gasped.

"Don't look at it," Missra warned him.

"Tell me what it is—do you know?" The merc sounded close to hysteria.

The thing must be huge, in that it nearly filled the hangar, nearly had no room in which to shift its position. Its great, hulking or crouching body was entirely composed of some seething substance, like restless cells that weren't quite working in conjunction with each other, weren't quite coming together … and maybe that was a good thing. In fact, the longer Missra stared at it, the more she began to suspect that if she saw that partly-amorphous, almost-tangible body up close, the restless components of which it was formed would reveal themselves to be those silvery strands like sea plants that she had witnessed on the other monitor.

As if the thing in the hangar had heard their voices, realized they were viewing it, it raised its head. What it had for a head.

Its head was more like an immense sea anemone, consisting simply of a nest of tentacles that not only writhed but seemed to lengthen then shorten again as they probed the air. These tendrils were like thicker, much longer versions of the densely-packed silvery strands of which the rest of the body was made.

The titanic entity seemed to meet Nichts' gaze, though it had no true eyes, for the clone suddenly gripped his head in both hands and doubled over with a strangled cry. It was as if a bullet had been lodged in his skull. Missra reflexively put a hand on his back.

"Yogthutu!" Nichts groaned through clenched teeth.

Missra reached out to the screen again, hoping to shut down the feed, though she was almost afraid to touch it … as if in doing so she might be touching that entity itself.

When her fingertips came in contact with the virtual screen, something like a powerful electric shock went through Missra's form and she was riveted there, eyes wide and mouth wrenched open. She juddered in place, paralyzed, unable to withdraw her hand from the screen. She remained fully conscious, however, and experienced the strange fear that she might be drawn *into* and *through* the screen at any second …

Then Nichts was throwing his body against her, as if to tackle her, and together they struck the floor of the power station hard. Nichts immediately curled up into a ball, clutching at his head and moaning again.

With the contact broken, Missra sat up and looked toward the virtual screen. Floating above her, it once again showed only blowing curtains of static, the feed of the vast entity and the hangar now gone.

Missra put out a hand to Nichts again, but he flinched away and whimpered so she left him there while she gathered herself back to her bare feet. The metal floor was cool beneath them. She smelled machine oil, and maybe a distant, pervasive hint of popcorn butter. Illusion made too, too real. Just like her.

Just like what they had seen on that screen.

"You made that thing, didn't you?" Missra called out to the ceiling. "Like those models you made to catalog all the different Old Ones. This isn't something that has come through, Devon ... this is something you designed. There *is* no Yogthutu."

At least—unlike all the impossibly ancient Old Ones—there hadn't been until now.

Fifteen
Vice

"You know this guy, Rex?" asked Gabriel Hounds. "You ever see him before—like, say, in your gun sights?"

Colin stepped closer to the corpse that lay sprawled between them. It was the body of a Dacvibese, one of many races of immigrants to the planet Oasis, who like all Dacvibese resembled an albino greyhound, with its pink goat-like eyes staring open in death. In life they were bipedal, though not in the habit of wearing clothing, but this particular Dacvibese would never walk on two legs again. A hole from a beam weapon had burned through the victim's chest and straight out the other side.

Colin and Hounds, a vice squad detective, stood over the corpse in the trashed, stripped and burnt-out shell of a convenience store that had been ransacked during some protest or other a year or two back. Near the store's entrance, a pair of uniformed forcers who had responded to the call were interviewing some kids who'd chanced upon the body while stealing into the store to get up to what kids got up to. The mostly empty, poorly-lit interior glowed with floating holographic graffiti tagged by various insignificant local gangs.

"Don't know any Dacvibese, personally," Colin replied. "But they smell almost as bad dead as they do alive, huh?"

"Have some respect," Hounds said. Gabriel Hounds was a human of Earth ancestry, a Black man with a perfectly bald head but metallic gold mustache and goatee, in a long deadstock-leather trench coat. Under present circumstances, Colin couldn't help but notice the detective had a single ultranet port implanted above his right ear. Hounds went on, "I happen to know this Dacvibese was selling purple vortex in this neighborhood, which is close to the territory of your boss, Jolly Bill. One might think Jolly Bill wasn't happy about the competition. One might even think he would send someone after this dealer, here, to remove that competition."

"I don't presume to know the thoughts of Jolly Bill," Colin said. "All I can tell you is I never saw this person before myself, let alone being the one who took him out. If you really thought it was me you'd be taking me in right now. I'm going to assume you just want my feedback, which is that he ... or was it a she?"

"He."

"That he was just robbed in a simple drug deal. No more than that."

"Would you consent to come down to the precinct for a truth scan, to confirm your innocence?"

Colin met Hounds' eyes. "No."

"Didn't think so." Hounds glanced back at the two forcers by the door to be sure they weren't looking this way, then in a lower voice said, "If Bill doesn't want us to lean on him about this, he might want to consider giving us some incentive."

Hounds nodded to his partner, Dolores Ipsum, who stood back a little from the two men listening quietly. Dolores—who Colin knew as Doll— was a small, attractive human woman with an expression as dark as her hair. In fact she put him in mind of Missra a little, which might have been why he and Doll had slept together and briefly tried their hand at a relationship after he and Missra had failed at theirs. But Doll had demons of her own, whether those had to do with her work or not, and things hadn't proceeded far or lasted long. Maybe it was simply because, despite their respective careers having allowed their paths to cross, those careers were just too much at odds with each other ... no matter how many bribes she and her partner took from the Jolly Bill syndy.

Doll averted her eyes from Colin uncomfortably, as if ashamed, glancing toward the interviewing forcers herself.

"I'll talk to someone," Colin said vaguely. You never knew when you were being recorded.

"Good boy, Rex," Hounds said. Unconsciously, he reached up to itch at the skin around his ultranet port. Its rim glistened a little, as if wet. "That's all I hoped to hear from you. Now, you should go before Homicide-Robbery gets here. I wouldn't want you to really be seen as a suspect, would I?"

"He still might have done it," Dolores Ipsum muttered, while keeping her face turned away.

"I know that," Hounds said, clapping a hand onto Colin's shoulder and smirking. "But it's just some punk dealer, and to be honest Homicide might not even bother showing up."

Colin's icy eyes caused the detective to quickly remove his hand.

Hounds walked away to confer with the forcers and see what they'd learned from the street kids, but Colin called Doll back to him as she started to follow after her partner. With a reluctant look she returned to Colin where he stood over the murdered Dacvibese.

"Doll," he said, "I have a question. Or … I guess I just want your thoughts."

"About what, Colin?" she asked, sounding unenthused about revealing any further personal thoughts to Colin ever again.

Colin hesitated, staring down at the corpse, reluctant to share his own thoughts. Then he looked back up into her eyes directly and said, "All this crazy stuff going on in Punktown. I'm sure you're seeing it. What do you people think is going on? What's being done about it?"

"Are you worried?"

"Shouldn't everyone be? I just thought you being a forcer, you might be privy to some details the media hasn't released."

"I probably know as much as you do. They say it's terrorists, using some kind of virtual virus, mainly through the ultranet. It triggers rapid physical mutations, or something like that. I don't know how. Me? I say people need to stay the hell off the ultranet for now, but you know how addicted the sheep are to that. It's worse than the poisons you Jolly Bill people sell."

Colin controlled himself from wincing, but it felt like he did inside. To test her, to see if Doll was holding out, he ventured, "I've heard a little gossip in the street, that it might have something to do with some cults that worship alien beings that they see as gods."

"Religious cultists? So like I say, sounds like terrorists. Hell, the Purple Jihad claimed responsibility, but no one's taking that seriously; they claim responsibility if it rains." Doll removed a pack of cigarettes from inside her jacket, tapped one out. She offered Colin but he shook his head. She pulled the little string that lit its end, took a thoughtful pull, then squinted into the smoke that unfurled as if to watch for meaningful shapes that might briefly take form. "You know, though ... they say that all over Punktown, the Bedbugs have been coming together to have these ceremonies. Of course, no outsiders allowed, so no one knows what it's really about—just that folks are noticing it."

Bedbugs was the nickname given to a beetle-like race that the Earth Colonies more formally called Coleopteroids. The Coleopteroids, while mostly keeping to themselves, had helped the Earth Colonies Network develop interplanetary and even limited interdimensional teleportation, thereby making travel by spacecraft all but obsolete. In return, they had been allowed to settle freely on colony worlds like Oasis. Their various religious sects and beliefs were not well understood, though it was known that some worshipped immense extradimensional beings called Gatherers. Now that Dolores Ipsum had brought this up, Colin found himself wondering if the Gatherers and Missra's Old Ones might be the same thing, or at least related.

"So what are people saying these ceremonies are about? Are they trying to call their gods here to Oasis?"

"Like I told you, nobody really knows what it's about. You know our government ... they don't want to press the Bedbugs in case they get called prejudiced. Though nobody really likes the Bedbugs. Nobody being me, at least. But anyway, what I'm hearing is that they didn't *start* this thing that's happening, but they're trying to counteract it. Or cast protections from it, or whatever. Who can tell with them? They're weird, the Bedbugs, you know? So advanced technologically, but then all involved in their secret religious stuff."

"Mm," Colin grunted.

Doll blew out a prolonged plume of smoke. "It's getting strange, but strange is the norm in Punktown."

"Listen," Colin said, before he could stop himself. "Like I say, I've heard rumors. One of these rumors involves a person who supposedly might have started this virus. Released it by accident."

Doll turned her head sharply, stared at him intensely. "Oh yeah?"

"If ... if I hear more, and if it sounds like valid information, and if I were to tell you about this person ... "

"If you did, I'd get that info to the right people to take it higher," Doll said.

"Thanks."

"Are you sure you don't have more info for me now? A name? You're acting funny."

"Maybe I'm just developing a conscience."

"I can see where that would be disorienting for you."

"Hey, you two lovebirds!" Gabriel Hounds called from beside the dead store's door. "I thought you two ended that farce a long time ago."

"You'd better go," Doll said. "In case, if they're bored enough, Homicide-Robbery do show up."

"I might be calling you," Colin said.

"Promises, promises. Same old Colin Rex."

Colin started away, but looked back to Doll and said, "Tell him to stay off the ultranet, too." He jerked his thumb over his shoulder toward Hounds. "What does he do in there?"

"I don't even want to know."

Having returned to his Razur, parked against the curb a few buildings down, Colin decided to give Missra a call on his wrist comp. Mostly just to test whether she could now answer such a call, as he imagined she would be. However, she didn't pick up. He gave it another try, waited a good while, but again no answer. So were her restrictions not entirely lifted? Then again, he had no real knowledge of what an advanced AI could and couldn't normally do.

Missra. An AI. Like those were two separate things. But he was still having a hard time putting them together. He thought that he always would. To deceive himself that Missra still lived on was to embrace the deception that Devon had created to apparently diminish his own guilt. He didn't want to share Devon's lie.

And yet … he knew Missra as well as anyone alive, he thought. And when he talked to the AI, where was the difference, except in the realm of physical states of existence?

What would she think about his impulsively speaking with a detective, even a minor corrupt one, about matters pertaining to their own investigation? About him possibly turning over what they knew to the authorities? Would Missra be sympathetic, and agree that things were getting too big for them to keep their knowledge to themselves, that they were in way over their heads, or would she be appalled?

Apparently he'd have to go find out in person instead of over his wrist comp. If seeing Missra at Devon's place could be considered seeing her *in person.*

Colin was about to start his Razur when he heard muffled voices outside. He looked through his passenger window and saw people standing on the sidewalk, despite the start of a rainstorm, staring up into the sky with some of them pointing. He crouched lower in his seat to follow their gaze … and saw the signs.

Sixteen
The Signs

Like anywhere in Punktown, signs and advertisements in profusion could be seen clinging to or floating above buildings. A portion of these were actual physical objects, at best illuminated by a light tube, but many were screens that could alternate their displays, or three-dimensional holograms. It was the latter two types that had caught the attention of pedestrians. These seemed to be glitching at the moment, though why so many individual and unrelated billboards and advertisements would be malfunctioning—when there appeared to be no power outage, judging from all the lighted windows in the buildings that supported these screens and holograms—wasn't apparent.

Despite the quickly worsening rain, Colin stepped out of his vehicle for a better look himself, shielding his eyes with one hand.

Strangely, every screen-type sign and billboard within the range of his vision, glowing against the wet grayness, now displayed only static. Even more strangely, every holographic sign or advertisement was undergoing another kind of disturbance. From the small, rotating striped cylinder floating outside a barbershop, to a sinuous dragon that had undulated above the entrance to a Chinese restaurant, to an enormous armored soldier running with an assault engine in his hands to advertise a vidgame, and a fish the size of a bus swimming above a box-like building's flat roof to draw attention to the sea food market within—plus so many, many more Colin could see from where he stood, stretching into the distance—all had transformed so as to show the same image. The same figure, if it could be called that.

The softly-glowing figure seemed to loom on two legs, but that was uncertain. A bit more coherent in form was a pair of multiply-jointed forelimbs, drawn up close to the chest. On the larger of the holograms it could be seen that the figure appeared to be covered in silvery scales or coarse hair, but with each scale or strand moving with a life of its own. Or was this covering the stuff from which its body was entirely composed, inside and out? For a head ... well, it had no real head, only a nest of tendrils, each of which seemed to be searching and peering in its own direction, sometimes lengthening only to retract again.

The head reminded Colin of the optical tendrils of a Tikkihotto. But more than that, it reminded him of what had dislodged and replaced Tam Vonner's head in Club Feel.

The pedestrians mostly were pointing at the largest of these local holograms, which had replaced the military vidgame character running in place. As if it heard their exclamations, the titan figure turned its body slowly toward a group of them, the tendrils at the front of its plant-like head stretching and pointing downward.

As it turned, every other hologram large and small turned identically, all of their movements harmonized. None of them made a sound, of course, but their silence was in itself chilling.

A waitress with long inky hair stepped out of the Chinese restaurant to see what the fuss was about, after someone had gone running into the establishment in terror. The hologram directly above her head, that had formerly been in the shape of a serpentine dragon, reached one of its forelimbs down to her. In unison, every one of the other holographic figures—whether in front of a shop, or hovering at a skyscraper's upper levels—reached down as well ... but it was only the one over the door to the Chinese restaurant that grasped the woman's hair.

Fortunately, before the three-dimensional projection could close its digits firmly the woman realized what was happening and jerked herself free. With a cry of terror of her own, she dashed back into her restaurant.

"What the blast?" Colin cried aloud.

Seemingly having heard him, as it straightened up with only a few strands of hair floating free from its grasp the hologram above the door to the Chinese restaurant angled its body in Colin's direction. All the others followed suit, including the colossus that had formerly been a running soldier.

Colin ducked down fast behind his Razur, low to the ground. He had the irrational impulse to draw his Revenant from its holster, but resisted. What was that supposed to do?

The one that had grabbed at the woman was obviously a hardlight holo, able to some extent to physically interact with its surroundings. He had no doubt *all* of them were. But how? These were just simple advertising holograms, projected by cheap lenses … nothing like the equipment Devon and Tam had installed in their apartments to manifest Missra. Had their capabilities been boosted somehow? Colin didn't understand the technology, but even if the power to these many individual and unconnected emitter lenses had been boosted, how could they accommodate and implement that power?

There was one thing Colin did understand. Two months ago, two Gibster 800 cryo-cooled encephalon computers had been stolen from Devon Tellick's former place of employment: Daedalus Data. Carried out under the arms of a huge stranger, though each weighed five hundred pounds. He remembered Verge telling him, *"Those Gibsters are so powerful, the researchers were bragging that they could use them to project a hardlight house of multiple floors that people could actually live in."*

Even if what Colin suspected was true, as strong as those stolen computers were their influence surely couldn't reach over the whole, great expanse of Punktown. If, however, they were not so terribly far away from this area …

The curious pedestrians had by now all vanished from the street, and it wasn't the pounding rain that had driven them off. Colin poked his head up a bit, squinted through the explosion of drops across the hood of his hovercar. He saw that the army of holograms had all turned away from facing, facelessly, in his direction. Instead, they seemed drawn to a helicar that was swinging down between two towers, presumably having spotted the anomaly from on high and moving in for a closer look.

"Don't," Colin muttered. "*Don't!*"

Clearly the many linked holograms represented a single sentience, but whether that sentience was malicious or merely curious Colin couldn't tell. All he knew was that as the helicar came swooping in, the largest of these local holograms—that soldier game character—leaned out suddenly and caught the vehicle in one extended hand or paw. The helicar might have broken free, had the tendrils that made up the thing's head not reached out, lengthening beyond what Colin had thought them capable, and lashed themselves around the vehicle as well. The figure drew the helicar closer to its body, and as it straightened up again its tentacles seemed to wind themselves more tightly around the vehicle, along with both arms now pressing the helicar to its chest.

The other holograms all mimicked these movements, though none clasped anything solid against their own bodies.

Then, red streaks of energy were streaming at the largest holographic entity as it clutched the helicar possessively, maybe not even realizing that there was a terrified occupant or two inside—though Colin suspected that was the very reason for its actions. He looked to his left and saw that further along the street, in front of that shell of a convenience store, the two forcers in their black uniforms and helmets were firing ray bolts at the thing from the service pistols they extended in both fists. Again, Colin didn't feel firing at this entity with handguns was going to accomplish much, but then what did he know about the vulnerability of hardlight holos? He was just concerned that their gunfire might strike the helicar instead.

He saw Doll and Hounds hanging back behind the two forcers with their own guns drawn, but perhaps wisely they refrained from joining in the fusillade. The kids who had discovered the dead dealer had already run off.

Then, an explosion snapped Colin's attention back to the largest of the holographic creatures.

He didn't know whether the giant had crushed the helicar too tightly against its chest, or whether the forcers' energy bolts had indeed struck the helicar, but either way the vehicle had erupted into a ball of fire. Small bits like shrapnel went flying in all directions, but the bulk of the ruined helicar dropped loudly to the street below.

And at the moment of the explosion, in a blink, the titan had vanished. It, and all the other holographic entities. The original holograms did not return to take their place, and the street became that much darker for the loss. In fact, all of the screens that had traded their advertisements for churning static went black, as well. Still, lights remained on in the buildings that supported these dead signs and billboards.

Colin rose up from his crouch behind his hovercar, his hair plastered to his head. He saw Doll and Hounds and the two forcers go running toward the smoking ruin of the helicar, as if there was any hope for its occupant or occupants.

He briefly considered going to join them, but what good could he do? What assistance, or even ideas, did he have to offer beyond what he'd already discussed with Doll?

All he knew was that this event, too, unquestionably was due to whatever it was that Devon Tellick was up to. And again, that if those stolen encephalon computers had caused the holo-emitters in this part of the city to all produce the same hardlight holograms, they had to be at least somewhere not too distant.

Seventeen
The Silhouette

Nichts had grown quiet, no longer moaning and whimpering, and Missra realized he had fallen asleep where he lay curled on the floor. She sat hugging her knees nearby. Occasionally she tried to will herself back to Devon's flat, or even Tam's, but continued to find herself unable to do so. She didn't know how much time passed, but she figured Colin—who wasn't the type to sleep for long periods at a time—by now had woken from his own nap to find her gone. Would he only assume she had withdrawn from view and gone inert? That thought wouldn't alarm him: he knew now that in such a standby state she was never so inert that she couldn't easily return herself to being *present*, so to speak, both to herself and others.

"Missra," said a familiar voice, and she flinched. Not for a fraction of a second had she thought Nichts had awakened and addressed her. She scrambled to her feet, swung around, and saw that large virtual screen had become active again. Except this time, instead of the hangar structure with its uncanny occupant, she saw another figure framed there.

This person was barely a silhouette, obviously seated in front of the viewscreen through which they communicated with her. Behind them was a room so shadowy that she couldn't guess its dimensions or features, lit only enough to make the figure somewhat distinct from its surroundings. She wouldn't have recognized this person by sight, but the voice had been unmistakable.

"Devon!" she cried. "My God—finally! Why haven't you answered me all this time? Why haven't you come back to look in on me, at least?"

"I'm sorry, Missra," said the silhouette. Maybe its voice wasn't entirely familiar? Maybe there was an odd, subtle distortion to it? Too deep … somewhat muffled? "I thought it was better for you not to be involved anymore in my research, to protect you."

"*Protect* me? Don't you think it's a little late for that?"

"No … I don't. You're still Missra, aren't you? I gave you back your *life*, and I won't lose you again. I left you where I thought you'd be safe, until later … when we could be together again."

"Do you have any idea what's been happening in Punktown? What happened to your friend *Tam?*"

The silhouette didn't answer. Hesitated. Then, that slightly distorted voice asked, "Who is that man on the floor?"

"A Blue War clone … a mercenary named Nichts. He and his friends wanted revenge on Tam for selling them corrupted programs … corrupted by a file Tam found in *your* library! I'm so sorry I had him look into that for me, because now he's *dead!* Do you realize that? Do you even care?"

"I'm … I'm sorry for that, but what I'm doing … it's so much bigger than one life. *All* life in our dimension is at risk. Have you forgotten that?"

"You have to do something about this virus! Even if it means stopping your research!"

"You know I can't do that." The head wasn't moving, Missra realized. Was this only an avatar? In any case, it went on, "How did you and that clone get in this room?"

"You didn't let him in? Nichts was at Tam's place, poking around in his system, and he said he felt drawn in."

"I'm … " The silhouette paused, seemed to struggle with its thoughts before it spoke again. "I admit I'm not in complete control of what's been happening."

"All the more reason to end your research! Shut it all down! Wipe it clean! All those books in your library!"

Again the dark figure ignored her, and instead said, "You two shouldn't be in one of my rooms. Sometimes … sometimes cracks appear, and I have to patch them up again. You both have to go back."

"Yes, please, let us out of here, but Devon … "

"I thought you understood me, Missra," that deepened voice slurred. Missra might have suspected he was on drugs, if Devon were into that sort of thing, but she knew he had always liked to keep his mind sharp and clear. Once upon a time, anyway.

"I understand how obsessive you are," she replied.

"It's the only way to have the strength to confront them. The only way any of us will survive."

"But you just said you can't control what's happening!"

"And that's the thing, Missra. If I can't teach myself how to control this simulation, how would we ever be able to control the real thing? That's the whole point of this, don't you see?"

"Your simulation itself has become too dangerous!"

"I need more time … "

"This whole city is running out of time!"

The silhouette seemed to sigh tiredly. "Missra, you two need to go now. I need to patch things up so neither of you can sneak back in here."

"Devon, wait—"

"I will see you again, Missra, I promise."

"Tell me where you are! Where you *really* are!"

"I told you, I'll come to *you*."

"Colin's looking for you!" Missra blurted. "He wants revenge for Tam, too! If he finds you before I do, I'm afraid he'll … he'll … "

"Colin, eh?" Did that weirdly slurred voice chuckle. "So you and Colin are talking again, are you? He wants to kill me, is that it? And you think that's about *Tam*, Missra? You don't think that's about you and me?"

"Devon, let this man go and bring me to you."

"Enough, Missra. I have to get back to work. I know things have gone awry, but believe me, I'm learning so much … "

134

"So tell me all about it! Take me there and show me what you've learned!"

"I love you, Missra."

Missra gasped, like a swimmer too long without air bursting to the surface, her eyes darting in wild disorientation until she realized she was standing in the living room of the old apartment she had shared with Devon. She looked to the sofa, hoping to see Colin still sleeping there, but he was gone.

Then, remembering Nichts, she glanced around for him, too, but again there was no sign, even in the other rooms. Of course: she recalled that he'd said he and his boss, Jornel Riggs, had returned to Tam's flat. It was into Tam's ultranet system Nichts had hacked.

With only a thought, Missra sent her presence to Tam Vonner's apartment, appearing there instantaneously.

Immediately, she caught sight of Nichts sitting at Tam's main work station, which—though he had further equipment in his bedroom and even on some shelves in the kitchen—dominated one entire wall of the living room. Even now the equipment was still active, readouts displayed on screens both solid and holographic, colored lights blinking and fluttering. His back was to her, but she saw the Blue War clone had pasted ultranet interface disks to both temples.

"Nichts!" she exclaimed. "Are you all right?"

At the sound of her voice, a bestial cry that seemed to shake the walls came from the bedroom. Startled, Nichts spun around in his chair, and Missra too whipped in that direction. For the first time she noticed how the sofa was badly burned, and how a blackened trail ran from it across the floor toward Tam's bedroom … from which, unknown to her, Colin's green plasma had spread after he had put one of the Ronin Security men out of his misery.

And now, as she faced toward the open bedroom door, a hulking shape appeared there, and at the sight of her came charging through.

The last time Missra had seen Jornel Riggs in this apartment, he'd shown her that his hairless head had sprouted glossy, ball-like tumors of various size, smaller orbs growing atop larger ones. Now, in a flash as he lumbered toward her, she saw how his mutation had progressed so much further. His entire body was covered in those same silvery, fleshy bubbles, some as big as melons hanging with their weight, extending down even to his fingers. At some point he had removed all his clothing to accommodate the growths, so bulky had he become with them. Only one eye barely showed through the masses that had obscured his face, but that single eye blazed with madness.

Who knew whether those growths extended even inside of him, into his brain? There didn't seem to be much left of the man's mind except for that madness, which because he had been designed as a warrior translated only into the primal urge to find an enemy, and kill it.

Missra stepped back, holding up her hands. "Wait!" she cried.

The mutated clone only gave another rumbling, phlegmy bellow as it kept shambling toward her as fast as it could manage in its deteriorating state. It reached out both its club-like hands toward her ...

Then, Riggs' misshapen head exploded, and split apart into flaps that flopped down about his shoulders, a thick silvery sludge running between the orbs clustered upon his chest and back. Much of that sludge had splatted against the nearest wall. A few drops had even struck Missra, but they ran off her quickly like mercury without leaving stain or wetness.

Riggs had stopped advancing on Missra, stood rooted in place for a moment, headless, before toppling sideways, giving a last convulsive shudder, then lying still.

Missra turned toward Nichts and saw he had risen from Tam's chair, still pointing his handgun at the fallen mountain of flesh.

"He survived the blasting Blue War," he murmured, "only to die by the hand of one of his own men. And all to save an AI he probably couldn't have hurt, anyway." He gave a sad chuckle, finally lowered his pistol.

"You did the right thing," Missra told him. "You ended his suffering."

Nichts nodded, holstered his gun. "Now it's just me."

"We should both of us leave this apartment and never come back. Too much has happened here. Nichts, if you want to avenge your friend—all your friends—you should help my people now."

The clone turned to her as he peeled the interface disks from his temples. "To do what?"

"To fight that thing you and I saw in the ultranet."

"Yogthutu."

"Yes. And whatever else might be connected to it. It has to be ended, and you might say my team is shorthanded."

Missra feared this suggestion would reignite the terror he had experienced in the ultranet, but Nichts surprised her when a smile slowly formed on his blue-skinned, camouflage-patterned face. "It would be good to have a real fight again. It's what I'm made for."

"There's only one other place I can appear in—I'm going to go there now. I'll give you the address, and you can meet me. I'll let you in."

"I'll be there," Nichts said quietly, casting a look again at that heap of fleshy spheres as grayish-silver porridge continued to ooze from its shattered remnant of a head.

Eighteen
Blue Warehouse

Colin was pushing his Razur the best he could through Punktown's congested streets, while inwardly cursing that Gabriel Hounds had summoned him so far from Devon's apartment only to confront him about a murder he was not only not responsible for, but knew nothing about. Not that he hadn't accepted orders in the past to eliminate competition for Jolly Bill.

Whenever his vehicle was forced to come to a crawl or even a full stop, he scanned through the net on the Razur's dashboard screen, looking for stories about the incident he had witnessed with the holograms. Nothing so far, but it was probably too soon for it to have hit the news, and he wondered too if people would even connect it to the mutation virus. He wanted to know how widespread the incident had been, seeing as how it had extended to the furthest reaches of his own vision at the time—though even then, that was only a fraction of Punktown. He also hoped to hear some discussion of what that event had been, and further hoped that it was being seriously investigated.

And then, a call came on his wrist comp, and he saw it was from one of Jolly Bill's captains—a burly, middle-aged Choom named Kad Paroon. On the wrist comp's screen Kad's ear-to-ear grin looked friendly enough, but Colin knew the man better than that. It was often Kad who called Colin on Jolly Bill's behalf, since their boss didn't trust communicating over devices no matter how much security tech they had in place.

"Where are you at, Colin?" the Choom asked.

"Stuck in traffic," Colin said.

"Can you get to the blue warehouse?"

Colin knew the place Kad was referring to. The syndy captain was too wary, himself, to be more specific about the address over the wrist comp's channel.

"I was just down that way," Colin said. The warehouse in question was only two blocks from the convenience store Hounds had summoned him to.

"Well get that way again. Or do you have someplace better to be?"

Actually, Colin did have someplace better to be—Devon's place, so he could tell Missra about what he'd witnessed. He'd tried a few more times to call her, and because she still hadn't answered he was becoming anxious to get back.

"This can't wait?"

"Colin … he'll be waiting for you there himself."

Colin understood what individual Kad was alluding to, also.

After a moment's hesitation he said, "I'll be there, but I need to turn around somehow in this traffic."

"I'm sure you'll manage." The Choom signed off.

Colin did manage, by turning the Razur into a side street and then through some others like it, to get the hovercar pointed back toward the area where the hologram event had occurred. And while doing so, he again tried Missra, and to his surprise this time she answered, her face appearing on his wrist comp's screen. AI or not, it was a vast improvement over Kad.

"Where have you been?" he asked her.

"I just got back."

"Back from where?"

"It's a bit of a long story."

"So tell me. Traffic is slow."

"Where did you go off to?"

"That's part of my own long story. You go first."

So Missra brought him up to date, right down to the fact that Nichts was presently on his way to Devon's flat to join her.

"And you trust him?"

"I do. I'll fill him in on everything we know once he gets here. And so now tell me your long story. It can't be any weirder than mine."

"I'll let you be the judge of that," Colin said.

Finally, as he wrapped up his account, he neared his destination. Colin noted that in the neighborhood of the blue warehouse advertising screens finally displayed their regular content, but every holographic sign was still out, as if every emitter had been overloaded by the incident.

Before signing off, Missra exhorted him to be careful. It was an unnecessary sentiment, but he appreciated it nonetheless.

The warehouse had formerly belonged to an adjacent, defunct factory now firmly sealed up against kids or the homeless intruding. It was a metal building with rounded-off edges, looking more like some retro spacecraft that had landed on the spot, painted with a glossy sky-blue paint, though that had blistered badly over the decades. Colin nosed the Razur through a gate in its surrounding barred fence, which was closed remotely after him, and halted the hovercar in a parking lot as cracked as a dried-up mudflat, though it sported a number of other vehicles. Those that weren't stripped husks belonged to fellow syndy members. From their number— four hovercars and two odd-looking vans—Colin estimated there must be at least a dozen people inside. He liked to have a sense of how many dangerous people there were in any place he walked into. Twelve would normally give him cause for concern, but he knew Bill's crew often met in this building to handle any number of business matters, or just to hang out.

Away from the old loading docks, a side door opened in the warehouse and another Choom—one of Kad's men—appeared there to gesture for Colin to come inside. The rain was tapering off, but this soldier upon seeing how soaked Colin was said, "Been swimming, Rex?"

Colin didn't dignify him with a response, and followed the Choom through a corridor lined with darkened shipping and receiving offices, until they stepped out into a large, high-ceilinged area that still contained rows of metal racks, though long empty of whatever pallets of goods they had once held.

Ahead of them he had spotted something strange. "What's that?" he asked the soldier who'd met him.

"A field hospital," said the Choom.

Now Colin understood those two odd vans in the parking lot.

In an open area of floor stood a cube formed from softly blue-tinted barrier fields, even floor and ceiling. Looking like some high-tech terrarium, this cube—which came to about Colin's chest—contained a number of four-inch albino salamanders, moving about bipedally. They were tending to the machinery that filled the cube, consulting monitors, a few seated at work stations. It was like a miniature version of the interior of Verge's ninetieth-floor apartment.

Verge …

One salamander creature was not bustling about, but lying flat at the center of the cube, encased in what looked like a block of greenish translucent gelatin. Perhaps it was due to the gelatin's tint, but this newt-being looked more grayish than its white-skinned fellows.

"Is that who I think it is?" Colin asked.

"He's in an induced coma," said the soldier.

While Colin stared into the cube, the environment it contained replicating that of its occupants' home world, Jolly Bill stood up from where he and several of his men had been sitting at two pushed-together cafeteria tables moved from a former breakroom, drinking coffee and nibbling fried dilky roots—a Choom favorite.

Bill came up beside Colin, with Kad just behind him, and gazed into the field hospital also. The mutant wagged his grotesquely long, horse-like head sympathetically, explaining, "When Verge took ill he let his people know, because they're not comfortable going to a regular hospital. You know, because of all this." He waved his hand over the artificial environment.

"This isn't a licensed operation, so they asked if they could set up in here, and of course I said okay. I look out for my people." He turned to Colin. "I'd do the same for you."

"It's that virus?" Colin asked, though he knew what it was.

"Yeah. His people are smart, you know that, so right now they've got him in a state where his mind is inactive. I guess that keeps the virus from worsening. Well ... he's mostly been inactive. Once in a while he comes out of it a little and says something."

"Do they expect him to live?"

"They're hopeful, but who can say right now?" Bill said. He was holding the end of a half-eaten dilky, popped it in his mouth. "Dilky? Coffee?" he asked while chewing.

"I'm good." Colin didn't take his eyes off the newt suspended like a fossil in that block of greenish gelatin.

"You have any idea how he got sick like this, my friend?"

"Who knows?" Colin said. "It's going around, you know. Tech people like Verge ... you figure they're putting themselves more at risk."

"Some of the things he's said when he became conscious for a bit were puzzling," the syndy boss said, thoughtfully chewing. "For one thing, he's said your name a few times."

"Yeah?" Colin didn't look at his boss.

"He's said another name, too. Does Devon Tellick mean anything to you?"

Now Colin did turn his head toward the mutant. "A friend."

"One of those two dead friends of yours, that you said Verge was helping you look into?"

"It does have to do with that."

"Why's he going on about it?"

"Probably just because he was looking into that so recently for me. It's on his mind." To steer Bill away from the subject, Colin said, "Hey, it's good we can talk now. I had a message for you from two forcers who called me to look at a stiff today."

It was hard to judge Jolly Bill's mood from his distorted face alone, but his tone became wary. "Oh yeah? And what's that?"

The two of them stepped away from the field hospital, toward one of the warehouse's inner walls. Kad followed but kept back a few steps discreetly. When Colin had finished relaying the message from Detective Gabriel Hounds, Jolly Bill slammed the flat of one hand against the metal wall so hard that it rang with the impact. Men still seated at the breakroom tables flinched, and even some of the salamander-beings inside the cube looked over, startled.

"Those dirty forcers think they can put the screws to me, just because I had a nobody dealer from a stinking gang of Dacvibese put down?" Jolly Bill rumbled. "Like we don't line their pockets enough? That's the problem with paying off forcers ... it just makes them thirstier."

"They thought maybe I did it," Colin said. "But they knew it was us."

"Well, blast them," Bill said. "I won't let those scumbags muscle me. I want you to take care of this, Colin. We'll send a message to all their dirty friends not to get too greedy."

"Take care of this?"

Bill snapped his eyes onto Colin in disbelief. "You too preoccupied right now, Colin? I get that you're worried about Verge, or your dear dead friends, but you don't know what I'm talking about? I want you to put those two dirty forcers down."

"Can't," Colin said.

Jolly Bill stared at him without speaking for a moment, and from the corner of his eye Colin saw Kad shift his position nervously. "What do you mean ... *can't?*"

"The other vice detective is a woman I was involved with."

The syndy boss absorbed this for a moment, then chuckled humorlessly. "You slept with a forcer, Colin? That's a dangerous business. Pillow talk can get you killed."

"We don't see each other anymore, but ... " Colin trailed off and shrugged.

"Okay, no, I get it. I'm not cold-hearted, as you can see." Bill gestured back toward the cube. "All right, then, forget the woman ... but you take out that Hounds fuck, you got it? That will send a good message to his partner that she can share with all her greedy friends in vice."

Colin held Bill's gaze for a few beats, then dropped his eyes and nodded mutely.

"I know that punk Hounds," Kad spoke up, to break the tension. "He's a real bastard. Won't be missed. The girl ... well, I guess I can see why Colin likes her. For a small-mouth." The Choom snorted uneasily, shooting for levity.

Jolly Bill kept watching Colin's face, his eyes hard in their far-spaced bony caverns. "In fact, I want his head left on a post wherever you end him, just for the full impact. With a few munits stuffed in his mouth."

"You don't think that's bit much?" Colin mumbled.

"I think it's just enough. Get it done right away, my friend. Every day I know that parasite is breathing I'm only going to get more steamed."

"Colin!"

The voice, translated and muffled, had come from a speaker within the cube made of energy barriers. Both Colin and Bill headed back that way, and Colin could already see Verge giving a little spasm inside the quivering block of gelatin. When they stood close looking in at him, he gave another jolt, and before quieting down again blurted one more word.

"Yogthutu!"

Nineteen
Regrouping

When Colin arrived at the apartment, it was to find the Blue War clone Nichts seated at one of Devon's old work stations with several holographic screens called open, examining the equipment Devon hadn't bothered taking with him to wherever he was now. Mostly, apparently, that which made Missra's existence possible.

Nichts swiveled around in his chair and nodded at Colin warily in greeting.

"We've met," Colin told him. "When I called your boss, LilBoyBlu."

"That was you, pretending to be your friend Vonner."

"Yeah." Colin addressed Missra. "If Verge and his nanomites couldn't find out where Devon is now from this gear, what makes you think this guy can?"

"I was our squad's tech man in the Blue War," Nichts spoke up defensively. "Reconnaissance, mainly. Finding the enemy was what I did."

Colin faced the clone again. "If you were the tech man, why are your buddies all mutated and dead but you're still, supposedly, unaffected?"

"I don't know that I'm unaffected, but looks like there's a randomness involved in all this, too. Who gets really bad and who doesn't. That's chaos for you."

Listening to this, Colin found himself squeezing his right hand into a fist. It was as achy as ever, or worse, the numbness in his fingertips so constant he was almost used to it.

Nichts continued, "That room Missra and I found ourselves in … she told you about it?"

"Yeah."

"That has to mean something. Why it looks that way, like it was part of a power plant. Why your friend Tellick would make a simulation like that. What we saw was probably only part of it."

"Part of a research site Devon's made in the ultranet," Missra said. "Having it look like a physical location makes it easier for him to connect to his real-world work."

"Unreality affliction and all that," Colin said. "The brain prefers things tangible."

"I still think there's more to it than that," Nichts mused aloud, swiveling toward Devon's system again. "I don't think that room was just some stock template. It felt too … specific. I think it's based on a real place."

Colin motioned with his head to call Missra closer to him. "I just went to see my boss, Jolly Bill."

"I was wondering why it took you so long to get here. What's going on?"

Colin told her about Verge. He didn't tell her about the job the syndy boss had assigned to him.

Missra put a hand to her mouth. "Oh, poor Verge! I hope his people can do something for him."

"So, in terms of tech wizards," Colin said begrudgingly, "I guess your friend Nichts is the best we've got now."

"Oh, Verge," Missra repeated, wagging her head. The concern in her eyes made her seem more compassionate to Colin than most living beings he'd known. Missra and Devon, always the do-gooders. So unlike him.

"Maybe if I could find that place again … " they heard Nichts say to himself.

"You mean, in the ultranet?" Missra said. "I'm sure Devon's safeguarded that site again, but even if you could get back inside, wouldn't you be afraid to?"

146

His back to them, Nichts was slow to reply, until he admitted, "I prefer my battles in the real world."

"We have that in common," said Colin.

Watching Nichts study the equipment, closing down one screen and opening another, Colin recalled that on the way here from the blue warehouse—and fortunately traffic had eased up a bit by then—he had been anxious to get back because he didn't like the idea of Missra being alone with a strange and dangerous man, in case he got it in his head to assault her. Then, Colin had remembered that this concern creeping in on him was ridiculous. For one thing, the Blue War clones had been designed to be without sexual feelings, lest they become distracted in their duties as soldiers … as too many birthed soldiers had been, taking blue-skinned Sinanese women as lovers, but usually taking them by force. Also, he had reminded himself of what Missra herself was. Her vulnerability was not her body as a woman, but if something should happen to the equipment that hosted her. Nichts wouldn't try sabotaging *that*, would he? In revenge for his own dead friends? Colin thought it best to still keep an eye on the mercenary, no matter how much Missra now trusted him.

Suddenly Nichts spun back to face them and Colin caught his breath, expecting some major breakthrough.

"Do you have food here?" the clone asked.

Missra pointed him toward the kitchen. "Of course … please."

Looking wrung out in addition to being hungry, Nichts got up from his chair and left the room.

Colin seated himself on the sofa, suddenly feeling wrung out himself, despite his recent nap. Missra came to sit beside him, and he was a bit startled at this; looked over to see the cushion depress somewhat under her bottom. Thinking of her bottom made him wonder if she could remove those same black garments she always wore, and he chased the thought away angrily. Chased away his memory of what she looked like without clothing. He didn't like how mush-minded he was starting to feel, and prayed there was no physiological reason for that.

He had rested his hands on the tops of his legs, his right hand still unconsciously squeezed tight, and Missra reached over to place her left hand atop his fist. He was torn between the impulse to recoil from her touch and a gratitude that pierced him deeply. He could feel some pressure there ... could feel the ghostly suggestion of her fingers curling around the ball of his fist as if to soothe the tension from it.

"Devon got you and Tam killed. I may have got Verge killed. And others are dying too while we flail around trying to find that son of a bitch boyfriend of yours," he said. "We need to go to the authorities, turn it all over to them."

"They're already investigating the virus."

"But if they had his *name* ... if they knew where it all *started* ... that could make all the difference!"

"Maybe. Or maybe it's Devon himself who needs to end this ... only him who can. I told you what he said to me. Yes, this ... this composite Old One he designed to study them has gotten out of control, but he's working on that!"

"You're just afraid the authorities will hurt him."

"I'm more afraid that you'll do that, actually."

Colin jerked his hand out from under hers and shot up from the sofa. "After all this, you're still in love with him!"

Still seated, a complex mix of emotions that could only be human showing in her large dark eyes, Missra replied, "I thought you said I was only some kind of clever illusion. How could I still love him?"

Colin started pacing, more quickly than usual when he was agitated, a state which in the past he had always managed to control. Before his reunion with Missra.

"You're right," he told her. "I am going to hurt him. I'm going to kill him. I told you that before."

"Then if Devon dies, what happens in the future if the equipment in this apartment fails? The equipment that maintains me? Then you'll have killed me, too."

148

Hearing them argue, Nichts appeared in the doorway to the kitchen munching on some frozen dilky roots that he had heated up. Colin saw him there and asked, "If this equipment that hosts her failed, could you repair it? Could you move it to another apartment, if you took these emitters here?" He gestured at the green glass orbs spaced about the room, up near the ceiling.

Chewing, Nichts shrugged. "I think so. Sure."

"We should take any gear associated with her that Tam had, too, so no one messes with it when we abandon that place," Colin continued, still pacing.

"Is it important to you that I continue to exist, Colin?" Missra asked, watching him from the sofa.

He halted his pacing to glare at her. "Yes! It is, okay? Yes!"

She nodded, the emotions in her eyes settling on a kind of sad warmth. "Thank you."

His wrist comp beeped, and he looked down at its screen. Read a text.

"What is it?" Missra asked him.

"That blasting Kad."

"Kad?"

"He works for Jolly Bill. They're pushing me to do … an errand for them. They want it handled right away."

"With all that's going on, you have to worry about that?"

He lowered his arm and said, "What am I supposed to do?"

"You're enslaved by him."

"I *work* for him." Colin started for the door.

"What—right now?" Missra said incredulously.

"I should just get it over with." He paused at the door to the apartment to look back at her. "Think about what I said, about giving up his name."

Then, he left.

Nichts pulled another dilky out of its crinkly foil package. They weren't nearly as nice this way as freshly deep-fried, but for him they seemed to hit the spot. "He's in love with you, isn't he?" he said.

Missra stared at the closed door. "Yes."

"And how about you?"

She lowered her head, not sure what to say. At last: "Once. Maybe still. I don't know."

Nichts nodded. "Guess I'm glad I don't love anybody, and that nobody loves me. It doesn't look pleasant."

Missra turned to smile at him. "Your friends loved you."

"Guess you could say that. Yeah … yeah, they did."

"And now you have new friends."

Nichts smiled. "Yeah. Guess I do."

Twenty
Transactions

I n the parking lot of Devon's apartment building, Colin sat in the dark of his Razur without having started it. Vice squad detective Gabriel Hounds appeared on his wrist comp's screen. In the background a loud sports game was playing on Hounds' home VT.

"Why are you callin', Colin *Wrecks*?" Hounds asked, drawing out *Rex* in such a way that Colin understood the joke. "I'm off duty now."

"I have what you asked for."

And he wasn't lying. In a secret compartment between the Razur's backseats and its trunk he always kept a duffel bag filled with emergency supplies in case he was ever on the run and couldn't return to his current residence: a spare handgun, a compact shotgun loaded with crystal shot, a burner wrist comp, and physical currency banded into bundles, which totaled ten thousand munits.

"And what's the quantity?"

"One, zero ... zero, zero, zero."

"Huh." Hounds smirked sourly as he contemplated this sum. "Not bad, I suppose ... for one person. And you'll give the same to Doll?"

"That's the quantity I was allocated," Colin said. "Why does Doll even have to know about this? You're the one who asked for it, not her."

"Sheesh," Hounds said, settling back in his living room chair to process this offer. "I guess neither of us is as loyal to her as we thought, huh? Okay, whatever, I'll take it. But man, pulling me out again tonight when I'm sitting here feeling like I've got the worst hangover ever … "

"Good. I want this over with," Colin said. Over with quick, just like Jolly Bill said. "How about we meet where we saw each other last time? I can be there in an hour."

"All right, Colin *Wrecks*. I'll see you in an hour, then."

Hounds signed off. Colin started the Razur.

Traffic had much improved as true night fell. The rain had ended but the still-wet streets dragged out and blurred the city's infinite lights and colors, made a flowing river of them. In the vicinity of Devon's building, at least, holographic signs glowed against the night unaffected.

Colin didn't know where Hounds lived; didn't know if the detective would reach the abandoned convenience store before he did.

The holograms were still out in that neighborhood.

He pulled his hovercar to a halt in an alley at the rear of the burnt-out store, startling a homeless person who poked their head out from a makeshift tent made from a tarp. Another peered out from behind a trash zapper that had long since malfunctioned, stuffed with trash it couldn't disintegrate. Colin emerged and the curious faces withdrew.

He pulled out the skeleton key card Tam had loaded with passcodes for him, not sure the reader at the metal back door would be functioning. It was. The reader beeped, an indicator went from red to green, and Colin eased the door open, hoping it wouldn't squeal. He had his Revenant out in one hand, in the other carried the duffel bag now only containing the ten thousand munits in bills.

Moving toward the front of the store, one stealthy step at a time like a tiger stealing up on its prey, Colin could hear Hounds' voice. So he had got here first, then, but had he brought someone with him?

By the multicolored glow of holographic graffiti, Colin could see the dead Dacvibese was gone, of course, and that the plainclothes detective was simply talking into his wrist comp. Colin was close enough now to make out the conversation.

"You were showering, okay?" Hounds was saying. "I didn't want to bother you! I only stepped out for a minute … it's about a case!"

Colin could even hear the other voice; a woman's. "You're meeting someone, aren't you, Gabe? I know you, you blasting liar!"

"Look, you talk to me like that and I won't give you something nice when I come home."

"Something nice, huh? You mean like your dirty dick, after you're done with your girlfriend?"

"Don't talk to me like that, woman!" Hounds all but shouted, his voice echoing in the gutted, blackened room. Colin saw the man press his right hand to the side of his shaven head, as if the loudness of his own voice had caused him a knife stab of pain. "Oh, God! Dung! This blasting headache I've got, and you're … you're … "

Colin began raising the Revenant to point at the back of Hounds' head. It looked like he wouldn't even need to bluff and pretend to hand over the cash. This was too easy, and he was grateful for that. A corrupt forcer … he wouldn't be missed, would he? Not even all that much by a woman he had apparently betrayed in the past. This was what Colin told himself, as he stole another step forward. He had no intention, though, of decapitating the corpse; he'd say he didn't have time, it was too risky, but he supposed he could spare a couple of munits to stuff in his mouth.

"God," Hounds cried, close to tears. Now he gripped his head in both hands, doubling over.

"What's going on, Gabe?" the woman could be heard asking from the wrist comp's speaker. "Are you coming, is that it? It sounds like you're coming, you bastard! She gets her kicks out of you calling me while you two are fucking, huh?"

"*God!*"

"I'm throwing your stuff out the window! Look for it in the street when you get back here, if you have the nerve to come back here, you cheating momfuck!" Then the woman ended the call.

Hounds didn't seem to notice—still doubled over, still clutching his head. With him doubled over like that, Colin had lowered his handgun accordingly. But he hesitated in pulling the trigger.

Did Colin crunch a pebble of broken glass beneath his foot? He himself heard nothing, but as if Hounds had detected such a sound he whipped around to face Colin directly, his eyes crazed with pain and his teeth bared and gritted. He saw Colin pointing the pistol at his face. He saw Colin still hesitating ... still not pulling the trigger.

"I have the money," he heard himself saying numbly. As he lowered the Revenant, in his other hand he held the duffel bag higher.

But Jolly Bill! part of his mind protested. What would Jolly Bill say?

Hounds had withdrawn his demand. Yes ... yes, that was it. Why take the chance of killing a forcer if Hounds had withdrawn his demand of a bribe beyond the customary bribes?

He'd never killed a law enforcer before. But it wasn't just that. He felt as if Missra, like some omnipotent being who could teleport anywhere, was in the shadows watching him at this moment.

"*You!*" Hounds croaked through his clenched teeth. "You ... syndy punk ... "

Colin saw a spurt of silver fluid from between the fingers of Hounds' right hand, bursting from the ultranet port above his ear. Only a second later, that one spurt turned into a steady gushing stream, arcing into the air. Colin had seen blood jet out of a person's head before, had *caused* blood to jet out of a bullet hole in a person's head before, but this was something different.

With an inhuman sound, part drawn-out groan and part rumbling growl, the detective dropped to hands and knees before he could advance one step toward Colin, as had seemed his intention. Colin watched, as fascinated as he was alarmed, as Hounds began to shake all over with violent convulsions.

Then, through peripheral vision, he saw someone floating at him from out of the shadows to his right. He cursed himself for letting down his guard, too engrossed in what was happening to Hounds. Though taken by surprise, he wasn't surprised to see this person was Dolores Ipsum, in both fists pointing a military-type Sturm assault engine at him, patterned in gray city camouflage.

"You were going to kill him," she hissed.

"I was only being careful. You see, I brought the money." He raised the duffel bag again.

"Liar!"

So Hounds had decided not to be disloyal to his partner, after all. Only five thousand munits apiece, then? Colin had underestimated him, and yet he had not entirely ruled out the possibility that he might bring Doll along for backup. If such turned out to be the case, he'd told himself on the way here, he'd still kill Hounds but spare Doll, advising her to take this as a warning to turn her back on her partner's execution and not step on the syndy's toes again. Otherwise she might find herself being anonymously reported for corruption, or—more likely—suffering an identical fate.

Doll took her eyes off Colin, if not the multiple muzzles of her powerful gun, and watched Hounds' full-body convulsions in horror. Foam was forming around his mouth, that geyser of silver fluid still streaming from his head.

"It's happening to him!"

Colin said, "You should get on your wrist comp and call emergency services."

"To do *what?*" Doll snapped, her eyes bulging with the beginnings of panic.

As if Hounds was shaking his own body apart, its atoms vibrating themselves undone, his back split open down its length. Thrusting up through the bioengineered leather of his trench coat were two membranes like the wings of a moth as it emerged from its cocoon, unfolding damply and dangling mucus-like strings. Bony structures like the struts of a bat supported these membranes, which quickly opened and spread themselves to full length.

"Shoot him!" Colin yelled.

Doll seemed reluctant to take her gun off Colin, who still held his own weapon down by his side. He was afraid if he raised it, that would trigger the forcer to open up on him.

"Do it! Hurry!" Colin urged her.

Hounds' unblinking eyes looked ready to pop right out of his head, until they did. From their sockets shot two long, multiply-segmented arms of metallic-looking chitin, with small pincers like those of a crustacean at their ends. These toothed pincers snicked at the air, as if searching blindly for something to grasp.

Then, abruptly, the entity that was emerging through the husk of Gabriel Hounds stood upright on its two hind legs. His chest was splitting open, a bulge forcing apart the flesh and the ribs there, which Colin took for a head emerging. Oddly, no blood flowed from this great wound, only more of that silver liquid pouring forth and splashing to the floor at Hounds' feet.

Still, Doll hesitated ... even though this creature was clearly no longer her partner. At last Colin swung his pistol up, and—without having to aim, the thing was so close to him—he fired it over and over, as the winged being started staggering toward him awkwardly on its newly-formed legs, sheathed within Hounds' own legs.

Finally, jarred from her paralyzed state by Colin's gunfire, Doll jerked her Sturm in Hounds' direction and opened up, herself. The military gun was set to fire solid projectiles on fully automatic, and as the weapon chattered quietly a string of holes advanced up Hounds' transfigured body, from his crotch to his throat.

Furiously, those two insect-like forelimbs began whipping around, in so doing tearing Hounds' head into two halves. The entity only made it a few mores steps toward Colin, however, as he backed off a few steps accordingly and concentrated his fire on that bulge pushing itself out through the dead man's chest. After having been struck with several bullets, the chitin covering of the emerging head finally broke apart like a shattered globe of stone. This was followed by an explosion of the soft, silver-gray matter that had been protected within the exoskeletal casing.

The thing that had been Hounds collapsed at Colin's feet, but Doll strafed it once again with her Sturm, a row of new holes opening up across its back.

"Whoa, whoa," Colin said, covering his face with one arm to protect it from flying muck. "Enough!"

They both lowered their weapons and stared down at the thing, Doll breathing hard with tears in her eyes.

"God damn it, Colin," she gasped. "God damn it!"

"Blasting ultranet junkies," Colin muttered.

She swung the assault engine at him again. "You didn't kill him because he changed—you came here to kill him anyway. You set him up for a hit! A *forcer!*"

"Listen, go easy, Doll." Colin lowered his handgun even more, down alongside his leg again. "I told you how it was ... believe what you want. But the important thing is, you're playing with fire provoking the syndy. Maybe that thing inside Hounds was making him crazy, but you went along with it."

"I should take you in!" she blurted.

"Don't make things bad for you, Doll. You won't be taking me in."

"Oh I won't, will I?"

He tossed the duffel bag in front of her.

"Take it. Ten thousand munits, all for you. In return, I walk. And I strongly suggest you never ask for, or accept, a payoff from Jolly Bill or any other syndy again."

Doll looked from Colin down to the bag, up at him again. She lowered the Sturm, lunged forward, snatched the duffel bag's handle and pulled it against her while still pointing the large weapon at him awkwardly in one hand.

"Then go!" she said. "Go before I change my mind!"

He considered, then, giving her one more gift besides the ten thousand. The name he had alluded to ... Devon Tellick. He could dump this whole matter into her lap, let her be the courier to deliver the information to the right people. If that happened, though, surely in no time the authorities would send forcers—even Colonial Forces soldiers—to Devon's old apartment, to descend upon the technology he'd left behind. In so doing, Missra would be ripped from that place … ripped from this reality. From existence. No, no, of course it was impossible to risk until Nichts had helped him get that equipment out of there.

"Turn your life around, Doll," he advised her as he started slowly, so as not to spook her, toward the front door.

"Maybe you should follow your own advice, Colin Rex," she said, still teary-eyed.

"Maybe I will," he said, and then he stepped back out into the night.

Twenty-one
Moving Day

When Colin returned to Missra, she asked him what had been so important that his boss had called him away into the night, but he wouldn't speak of it. Instead, he expressed the concern that had kept growing in him on the ride back ... that if people from the government somehow traced these events back to Devon on their own, they would descend on his apartment and the processes that enabled her to exist would be at risk.

"Right now," he said, "I want to take Nichts with me back to Tam's one last time, to remove those emitters, like I said." As before, he gestured at the emitters spaced around Devon's apartment. "I'd rather we take those to install in my place, before we mess with things here. That way if we screw it up we still have the main system here to work with. If we're successful, only then will I feel safe removing the equipment from in here, and walking away from this flat, too."

"That could take hours. You two are tired."

"I'm good," Nichts said, sipping a coffee.

"He's good," Colin said.

Back in the Razur, before starting the hovercar Colin leaned over the dashboard and pinched the bridge of his nose.

Having slipped into the passenger's seat beside him, Nichts looked over and asked, "You okay? You want me to drive?"

"Nobody drives my car," Colin said. "It's just a headache." Then he sat up, realizing what he'd said. Just a headache? He could only hope so. His right fist squeezed its steering stick. As he finally started the vehicle, he nodded at the unfinished coffee in Nichts' hand. "Don't spill that in here."

Night was becoming increasingly still, though only by Punktown standards. Punktown was never at rest. As Colin sped through its streets Nichts set his cup down in a holder and slipped into the restraining belt he'd neglected until then.

On the way, without getting into what he'd seen earlier that night in the ruined convenience store, Colin discussed the various mutations people were reporting and the kinds of changes taking place ... such as to Nichts' deceased boss, Jornel Riggs, and his other companions.

"That monster Missra and you saw in the ultranet might just be a creation of Devon's, a model he made to study these Old Ones. The thing I saw, too, with the corrupted holograms ... "

"Yogthutu," Nichts said.

"But the things coming out of these people, like my friend Tam, are no illusions ... they're real, physical entities. But are they really only one creature, one Old One that's trying to see which form works best to enter our dimension, or an endless horde of them? Beings of all types?"

"What I'm thinking about," Nichts said, "is how powerful Devon's creation Yogthutu is. A combination of different Old Ones. You see how real Missra is. Well, we know Tellick is using two blasting Gibster computers to power the emitters that project Yogthutu. Imagine how much more *real* he is than her."

"But Missra has *memories*. That makes her more real, in the end."

"Maybe. Or maybe Yogthutu has his own kind of memories, too. From all the books Tellick owns, all their content in his system. In effect, Yogthutu might have the memory of multiple alien gods ... millions of years worth of memories."

"Jesus," Colin said under his breath.

"So, who knows what abilities, what powers, a being like that could have. Even an artificial being. For all we know, these physical mutations we're seeing aren't from the Old Ones themselves. They might be too trapped in those prisons Missra talks about to do anything to return to our dimension on their own. Who knows, the Old Ones might all be dead for good at this point in time. But Yogthutu might be trying to give himself a physical body, and that's what we're seeing with the mutations. Each mutation is another attempt by him to manifest here in a biological state. Maybe he's trying different forms to see which works best ... referencing those books in Tellick's library, and the various creatures they describe. Or else, maybe these creatures appearing in our world are all just different parts of one gigantic being, that are supposed to combine in the end like all the organs and limbs of his body."

"God forbid that body should ever assemble."

"Don't talk about gods to me, please," Nichts said. "People needing their gods is what got us into this mess. I'm glad I'm a clone, made by birthers like you. At least my people can kill their gods."

Colin gave the former soldier a look.

They arrived at Tam's building to find a forcer helicar resting on the pavement outside the front door, its dome lights rotating, throwing waves of red and blue light across the building's face. For a few moments, with the Razur idling an inconspicuous distance away, the two men looked out at the vehicle.

Nichts asked, "You think the neighbors finally complained about all the commotion going on in Vonner's place?"

"I doubt it ... it's soundproofed."

"What do we do?"

"We act like we live there." Colin opened his door.

In the lobby, two forcers in black uniforms and beetle-like helmets were speaking with a youngish woman in a bathrobe, who was hiccupping with sobs and holding the side of her face, which appeared red and swollen. As Colin and Nichts crossed toward the elevators, both forcers turned their heads mechanically and watched the men with similar hard, scowling faces, despite one being a Black woman and the other being a wide-mouthed Choom. Colin felt their gaze trying to penetrate him, but he ignored them as they waited for one of the two elevators to descend.

When they were finally in one of the cabins and its door slid shut, Nichts let out a sigh. On the holographic screen, Colin hit the key for the thirtieth floor.

Colin again used the spare key card Tam had given him, and opened the flat's door to a terrible stink. Both men were well acquainted with the smell of decaying corpses, but this was more than that.

In the living room, the heap that had once been Jornel Riggs was liquifying, the countless spheres of which it was made leaking and deflating, a viscous pool of silver-gray fluid turning the carpet around it into a marsh. Colin didn't know how the sight of this might be affecting Nichts inside, but the mercenary seemed to purposely ignore the remains and went straight to his work, carrying the box of tools Colin had taken with him from the Razur's trunk.

Before removing the glass emitters from the walls, Nichts had carefully measured their distance from each other using an application on his wrist comp, and had taken still images of Tam's setup as well. Lastly he disconnected several units from Tam's computer stations, and Colin helped carry them. On their way out, before they shut down the lights, Nichts finally spared a look back at that nearly formless mound on the floor.

"You'll be avenged, sir," Colin heard the clone mutter.

Then, it was on to the subterranean region of Punktown, Subtown, and Colin's own flat. When he let Nichts in through the metal hatch he had for a door, he gestured around the sunken living room and said, "Sorry ... the walls here are metal. Might be a pain to install the emitters."

"Nah," Nichts said, nodding at the room in approval. "I like it. It works. It reminds me of being inside some old warship. That was something I missed out on ... before my time as a soldier. Space battles."

Colin rested the unit he'd been carrying on the chair positioned in front of the one small desk he used as his own humble computer station. Then, slowly, he turned to face Nichts.

"A warship," he repeated.

"What?" Nichts said, setting down the items he carried on the sofa. "What about warships?"

"Missra said what she saw on the screen … the thing you saw, too … the hologram of Yogthutu. It was in a building that looked like a hangar."

"Yeah … "

"And that room you both were in, that you said looked like the simulation of a power plant. Could that have been part of some old starship's engine room?"

Nichts' eyes widened.

They both said it at the same time.

"Phosnoor Shipyard."

"Of course," Colin said. "Phosnoor Shipyard isn't far from the place where I saw that event with the holograms."

"You want to go there now, have a look?" Nichts asked.

"Not yet—let's not go half-cocked. I want to get this system installed here first, so Missra can join us … fingers crossed."

"Got it."

Colin helped Nichts install the holo-emitter globes throughout his flat, using a beam drill to burn into his metal walls at the various X points the clone had marked about the central living room and adjacent rooms. He only hoped the lower ceiling in his flat didn't adversely effect things. When they were done with that, after a bit of sweat and swearing, Colin carried his kitchen table into the living room, placed it beside his little computer station, and Nichts began setting up the relevant units from Tam's comp station there.

"While I'm doing this you could grab some sleep," Nichts offered.

"Can't sleep at a time like this. My nerves are on fire. But I will grab a pain pill and a shower … change my clothes."

Nichts twisted around to meet his eyes. "Still got that headache?"

"Stress … too many pills to keep awake … too little food."

"At least eat something."

"You're as bad as Missra."

As he stripped down in the bathroom a call came on his wrist comp, and he picked up the device from where he'd set it on a corner of the sink. From its screen, that familiar Cheshire Cat grin belonging to Kad Paroon.

"Did you take care of that hungry dog, Colin?" Always careful with their wording, in case listeners might get past their security software.

"It's done. I didn't take the top off, though. It got weird. He changed."

"Changed?"

"That virus thing. He changed."

"Raloom!" Kad hissed, uttering the name of a Choom deity. "But it's done? And no one came with him?"

"Nope. Wanted it all for himself."

"Good, good. Let that be a lesson to those blasting stray dogs that get too hungry. You look like you're getting ready to fuck, or take a shower, or both. I'd better let you go before I get too excited seeing you without a shirt, pretty boy."

"I think you'd better."

The call ended, much to Colin's relief. As he showered, he thought it best to have something to eat next as Nichts had suggested. Having changed into fresh clothes, he stepped barefoot out into his living room to be greeted by Missra, standing there smiling. Behind her, seated at the new work station with its gleaming buttons and holographic screens, Nichts was also smiling, proudly.

"Well," Missra said, "that was easy. I'm grateful for the change of scene."

"Welcome to your new home," Colin said. "Now ... we've got something to tell you."

"What is it?"

"Phosnoor Shipyard," Colin said, watching her face for the reaction.

Twenty-two
The Shipyard

P hosnoor Village was one of the worst ghettos in Punktown, along
with such neighborhoods as Tin Town and Warehouse Way. Whereas
Tin Town's populace mostly consisted of mutants, Phosnoor Village's
denizens were primarily Choom—and Colin knew Jolly Bill had recruited
Kad Paroon and other Choom in his crew from that lawless area.

The outermost edge of this ghetto flanked the Phosnoor Shipyard
along one of its sides. On its opposite side lay what remained now of the
Paxton Spaceport, greatly reduced in size over the past decades as long-
range teleportation had slowly replaced spaceflight. There were, however,
still those civilizations that continued to rely on spacecraft, so the spaceport
had not been eliminated completely.

Once, the shipyard was where spacecraft had been taxied in for
maintenance and repair. As they became obsolete, however, these grounds
had become a spaceship graveyard, where some of the decommissioned
vessels were scrapped for parts while others languished like bizarre haunted
houses. Eventually, the interiors of three of the largest ships had been
subdivided into inexpensive apartments. Colin knew this because he had
once accompanied one of Bill's dealers to a converted old hospital ship
from the Red War—named the Caduceus, he recalled—to conduct some
business, acting as the dealer's bodyguard.

Though a number of these craft had been put to good use, there were
still those that just squatted there on the extensive grounds, their bulks

looming darkly. Meanwhile, beyond the graveyard and behind a high security fence, an occasional smaller craft of one alien type or another could be seen lifting off from—or coming in for a landing at—what remained of Paxton Spaceport.

Not to mention, there was also a row of large metal hangars, with curved roofs, that lined one end of the shipyard beyond a strip for taxiing. Colin and Nichts looked through the windshield at these hangars now, from where the Razur was parked on the ghetto side of the shipyard. By this time, another day was breaking in Punktown, the sky taking on a watery orange light.

"Would he have rented a space in one of them," Nichts asked, "or just broken in and set himself up on the sly?"

"That would be risky," Colin said. "If someone who cared enough discovered him and threatened him to leave, that would disrupt Devon's research. He wouldn't want that. He doesn't even want Missra disrupting him, no matter how much he pretends to still care."

"So he's renting. Guess it might not be too expensive, though. I'll bet a few of those hangars, if not most, are sitting empty. But he has to have access to a lot of power to be running those Gibsters. How does he afford that?"

"Maybe he's illegally tapped into the spaceport's power. He's figured something out. He's Devon."

"Hang on … the power plant. I mean, the engine room. Is he tech wizard enough to have powered up one of the old dead ships nobody's using?"

Colin turned to Nichts. "I bet that's it. He's using a hangar *and* a ship … the ship for a power source. But yeah, that does seem a bit much of a feat even for someone of his skills."

"Like I thought … the ultranet site I saw mirrors a real place, so he can manipulate the controls of the real place remotely from the ultranet. Man, if only he'd put these skills of his to good use."

Gazing out through the windshield again, Colin said, "He thought he was. No harm in that … until there is. At that point you have to know when to back off. Thing is, Devon doesn't back off."

"Neither do we," Nichts said.

"The ship he's using isn't in the hangar where you saw Yogthutu … you would've seen it," Colin mused. "It's either in another hangar, in which case he's renting two, or it's one of these other ships we're seeing outside."

"If so, it wouldn't be far from the hangars," Nichts said. "Maybe before we move in for a close look we should do some interviewing."

"Probably wouldn't hurt."

Colin's wrist comp notified him of a call, and when he saw it was Missra he wasn't surprised. Her face on the device's screen appearing worried, she asked him, "Are you there yet?"

He filled her in on what he and Nichts had theorized.

Missra said, "Can you leave communications on between us, so I can hear what's happening? I promise to mute myself on my end, so I won't make noise in case you're sneaking around."

"Okay."

"And Colin … please … if you can, just talk to him, will you? Can you promise me the first thing you'll do is simply try to reason with him?"

A tick of silence, except for the whine of a saucer-like craft rising from beyond the fence that separated the shipyard from the spaceport. Then at last, Colin grunted again, "Okay."

Nichts pointed through the windshield. "See that? Last hangar on the right?"

"I see it," Colin said. "It's open. That wouldn't be him."

"But there's activity inside. Maybe they know something."

"Okay … let's go." Colin nodded at Missra on his wrist comp as he got out of the car.

Colin carried one pistol in its holster under his suit jacket, the other tucked in his rear waistband. Nichts' long, waterproof duster enabled him to hide Colin's shotgun pretty well. If anyone should catch a glimpse of it, well, this was Punktown. It wouldn't seem all that unusual.

In the long row of hangars, the last one on the right had its roll up front door retracted. The closer the two men drew to the structure, walking between the bulks of derelict ships—vessels both refurbished for new purposes or forgotten like mountains of junk—the more clearly they could see the last hangar on the right was being used as a garage. Two modified hovervans rested inside, with spaces for more that had apparently gone forth on whatever their missions were.

"Those look like food trucks," Colin said.

"Hold me up," Missra said from the wrist comp.

"You said you'd stay muted."

"Right—sorry. From now on."

Colin lifted and angled his arm for her to see.

"Food trucks," she said.

"Mute," Colin told her.

They came close enough finally that Colin could see the van nearest to the hangar's wide opening sold a variety of foodstuffs made from insects. The van's open side panel revealed clear cages in which swarmed several different types of live insects and grubs that could be cooked any number of ways on the spot. Judging from the placards on its sides, the other van apparently sold falafel, shawarma, and the like, but it was shuttered at present. One human worker of Earth ancestry was restocking the insect van, from containers he had wheeled over on a cart from some storage room at the back of the hangar where offices had one been.

This worker noticed them approaching and paused from his duties, warily setting down the container he carried, possibly filled with more writhing beetle grubs. He said, "Sorry, we're not open right now. Our breakfast truck is probably over at the spaceport, if you want to go there."

"Not hungry," Colin said. "I was just looking for a friend I heard might be living here at the shipyard. Devon Tellick … you know him?"

"No, sorry," the worker said, still looking guarded. His eyes kept flicking warily to the silent Blue War clone with his camouflaged face and long black duster. "Doesn't ring a bell. Most people here live in one of those big old Colonial Forces ships." He motioned back toward the maze of spacecraft the two men had woven through to get to the hangars. "Unless he's homeless. Homeless folks get into the junk ships."

Colin persisted. "He's doing some research here, is what I heard, so he's probably in one of these hangars. He's probably making use of an old ship, too ... also for his research. Ring a bell now?"

"Oh, wait," the man said. "Is your friend this huge guy who always wears a hat, like a fedora?"

Colin and Nichts exchanged a look. "A mutant?" Colin asked.

"I don't know if he's a mutant or not. Nothing personal, but I don't want to get close enough to find out. So is your friend a mutant?"

"No, I think you're describing a ... a friend of our friend."

"Well anyway, yeah, that would be the last hangar on the other end." The food truck worker pointed off down the line of humped metal structures. "I've heard people talk about that, uh, friend of your friend coming and going. And now that I think of it, I've heard people complain sometimes they hear loud humming sounds coming from inside that last hangar, too. One guy told me it makes his head hurt something fierce when that happens. So I guess that's the one?"

"Sounds about right. Thanks," Colin grunted, and he and Nichts turned away.

"Now what?" Nichts asked. "We just go on up to the bay door and knock?"

"No," said Colin. "We look for another door and let ourselves in. He's not going to be answering any knocks."

In dawn's gloom and from a distance the hangars looked as though they were pressed cheek to cheek, but closer up they revealed themselves to have narrow spaces between them, and in these alleys were doors set into each hangar's flanks on either side, so as to permit people to enter or exit even if the great front doors were lowered in place—as they were on every other hangar but the one being used by the food truck fleet. Colin and Nichts saw that some of these alleys were choked with trash or old ship parts on pallets, and that the long sides of the hangars were slathered with graffiti both painted and holographic. In one alley, two dirty-looking little Choom children who apparently had no time for school were scavenging through the debris, either in play or to help support their families, and they glared at the adults defensively as if daring them to shoo them away. The men kept walking.

"I doubt my skeleton card will work," Colin said, raising his wrist comp so Missra could hear him as well, "but I'll try it anyway."

Even before they came up on the last hangar they took note of a spacecraft standing directly across from its front, itself the last in a row of wildly different vessels, some not of Earth origin. The ship in question was boxy in shape behind the more rounded bulb of its cockpit, but Colin couldn't guess what particular purpose it had once held. "Military, do you think?" he asked Nichts quietly.

"I doubt it. No guns that I can see. Looks roomy ... probably for delivering cargo."

"What's it's name?" Missra asked. "I can look it up on the net."

"Damn it, Missra," Colin hissed.

"Sorry ... but I heard you guys chatting away."

"It isn't important," Colin said. "Anyway, it's pretty old. And look." Again he angled his arm so Missra could see what he was indicating: the clearest proof that they had found what they'd come for. Socketed into an open panel in the ship's underside, near its tail end, was a sheathed cable as thick as Colin's thigh, running across the space between the ship and the hangar. The cable continued on through a hole made in the structure's face, low to the ground and to one side of the roll up door.

"It's subtle, but I can feel the vibration in the air," Nichts whispered. "It's making my teeth hurt."

Colin jerked his head toward the alley between this hangar and the one that preceded it, and they slipped into the shadows there where the last dregs of night clung. Right away they saw how the alley had been cleared of any obstruction. As they came up on a side door, Colin fished out his skeleton key card while Nichts swung the shotgun out from under his coat and stood ready.

"It could alert him if it fails," Nichts whispered.

"Can't just kick the door down. If it fails but it doesn't alert him, we stake out the place and wait for him to poke his head out."

"If he ever *does* come out."

Colin held his breath as he passed the card over to the reader. The door control's red indicator didn't turn green; there wasn't even the bleep of a failed attempt.

Whether there had been the sound of an alert on the other side, or whether a camera eye was installed in the reader or elsewhere nearby and they just hadn't spotted it, Colin didn't know—but suddenly the door slid open as if there had been a delayed reaction, and the arm of a giant shot out from the murky interior. Its gloved hand snatched him by the front of his jacket, and hauled him into the hangar so violently that his feet all but left the ground.

Twenty-three
Golems

Colin was flung into the hangar with such force that he had to go into a shoulder roll to spring to his feet again. As he spun back toward the door, tearing the Revenant from his belt holster, he saw that the giant in its floppy-brimmed hat and trench coat—which despite being oversized, was stretched to bursting across the figure's immense back—was already confronting Nichts. The figure blocked Colin's view of the mercenary, but he heard Nichts' shotgun blast the oncoming giant straight in the chest.

And yet, the giant kept coming, stepping out of the hangar into the little alley and forcing Nichts backward. The Blue War clone got off one more ear-clapping discharge from the combat shotgun, again point blank, before the weapon was swatted out of Nichts' hands. He cried out in frustration and fury as the giant caught hold of him, spun him around and pressed Nichts against its chest as if to restrain a child having a temper tantrum. Then, the giant wheeled around again to step back into the hangar ... using Nichts as a shield. Colin had already been reluctant to fire lest he strike Nichts—especially since the Revenant was loaded with devastating green plasma capsules—and now he had to be doubly cautious. He saw how the giant had one black-gloved hand clasped around the front of Nichts' throat, and had no doubt it could crush that throat if it closed its fingers.

Nichts' second blast from the shotgun must have been higher up, in the giant's neck and lower face, because a torn flap of the wide, pale chin now hung down. Also, though the fedora was pulled low and shadowed the stranger's eyes, Colin could now get a better sense of its face. He didn't doubt the face was made from real skin … but it was not living skin.

Not a mutant, then. A robot. A robot wearing a dead man's mask. Colin might even have thought, in that moment, that it was Devon's face— that Devon had transferred his consciousness into this machine—except that he could tell it was not *that* man's face, however much this preserved mask was distorted, stretched as it was to mostly cover what passed for the automaton's own countenance.

"Be careful, Colin," said a voice from a speaker. A familiar voice. "I honestly don't want to hurt you or your friend."

"Devon?" Colin heard Missra exclaim from his wrist comp. He had to lower his gun for a moment so he could disconnect their open call. He hoped Devon hadn't heard her; this was between the two of them now. And Nichts.

"Is he one of your gangster buddies?" The voice from the speaker seemed to sigh in disappointment, as if judging Colin for his adult life in its sordid entirety.

"Don't hurt him!" Colin called out. "He's only here to help me!"

"Help you? Help you hurt *me?* Is that what you're up to, Colin?"

"Why would you think that, unless you know what you're doing is wrong?"

"Because I know you. All you're good for is doing bad. To think I once liked you … but I suppose I felt obligated to, because Tam liked you. And Missra … oh yes, Missra definitely liked you, too."

"You got them killed!" Colin couldn't stop himself from bellowing with the full force of his anger, his voice echoing in the hangar's cavernous space. It was mostly empty, he saw, aside from a few handcarts bearing equipment, pushed off to the sides. He assumed that if Devon wasn't actually in that boxy old vessel across the way, then he had to be in those offices at the rear of the hangar. Their windows were either blacked out or the rooms were in darkness; from here he couldn't as yet tell.

Another detail he had picked up on was that green glass holo-emitters,

173

like the ones that enabled Missra's hardlight form to manifest, were spaced along the hangar's walls at the point where they began to curve into the high ceiling with its web of support joists. Except, there were many more such glass orbs here than there were installed in Devon's and Tam's old apartments.

Nichts tried to curse through his gritted teeth, but the effort caused the robot to close its fingers a fraction tighter around his throat and he only choked instead. Looking back to the robot, keeping the Revenant pointed toward its dead man's face, Colin at last became conscious of a familiar smell. The smell of a corpse. And, he noticed that rivulets of viscous, blackish fluid were running down the giant's legs. Colin might have taken it for something like hydraulic fluid, released by the shotgun's projectiles, except for that vile smell of decomposition.

"Tell that machine to let my friend go, before it strangles him!" Colin yelled.

Though the lips of its mask didn't move, the robot said, "I. Will. Not. Allow. You. To. Stand. In. The. Way. Of. Yogthutu."

"Shh, Golem, please let me handle our guests," Devon calmed the machine, whose voice—despite having no inflection—had sounded decidedly threatening. Devon explained to Colin, "I call him Golem. His model number is 6013-M. You see? Golem. He's remarkable. Do you want me to tell you about him?"

"Look … "

"When I managed to get into that old hauler across the way, and poked around to see if I could access its engines as a power source, I discovered Golem. He used to be one of several lift bots to load and unload cargo. A really nice model, with an encephalon brain, no less! A sin to just leave them behind in that old tomb. Unfortunately, the brains of the other two had decayed over time, but I was able to jack into Golem's mind and reactivate him. Well, in all fairness, after I sparked him up he did most of his resuscitation himself. In fact, it was *him*, more so than me, that got the ship's engines fired up again."

"So after that feat he just became your errand boy."

"I see him as a true assistant. But yes, he is willing to go out and gather supplies for me." Devon chuckled, as if proud of a growing child. "He isn't afraid to use public transit … though we prefer that he doesn't go at rush hour, if you catch my meaning."

Colin's wrist comp was beeping, but he ignored it, muted the alert. "And he wasn't afraid to get into Daedalus Data—using a copy you made of your old key card, I imagine—and steal two super-expensive Gibster computers. Where are they now, by the way … in the back there, with you?"

Devon ignored the question, and went on, "Because Golem's mind is mostly a bioengineered organ, when I connected him up with my system to revive him—utilizing some techniques I happened to have learned in my days at Daedalus—something unusual happened. He was apparently influenced by my research. It was something like what Tam unintentionally released when he messed around in my library so recklessly."

"A virus."

"Whatever it is, I don't understand it exactly, but Golem quickly began to take on something like real life. I could tell he was interested in … I'd say actually *enthusiastic* about my research. He has told me as much, and has repeatedly vowed to do whatever he can to bring my aims to fruition. Unfortunately, there have been some, ah, unfortunate aspects to his conviction that he too is an actual living being. That is to say, you may have noticed his face. And the human organs that he's stuffed into gaps in the front of his body. But I promise you, Golem didn't kill the man he took those things from! He found a homeless man in the alley outside our hangar one night, who'd died from an overdose most likely. Golem took those props from him. I didn't try to dissuade him. I found it rather sad and touching, really."

"*Props?*" Colin said.

"Well, I'm afraid I've been going on too long. I suppose in a way it's good to talk to another person again … aside from Golem, that is. But I have to ask you once more: what is it you and this soldier came here for, Colin? Why have you been hunting me? Surely you can't really blame me for what that cult did to Missra—we were lured into a trap! And what happened to Tam is *exactly* the kind of poisonous threat I've sought to protect this world from! Our whole plane of existence from!"

"What I came here for is to try to get you to stop doing whatever it is you're doing to make that ... that Yogthutu thing more and more real. I promised Missra I'd talk to you, so here I am—talking. Why don't you set my friend Nichts free while we have this civilized little discussion?"

"Because Golem appears to be the only thing stopping you and your friend from using those guns you came in here with. Despite whatever empty promises you made Missra. Like I told you, Colin—I know you. And you see? You don't even understand what I'm accomplishing with Yogthutu, as I rather playfully dubbed him, and why."

"So why don't you enlighten me? But my friend might die while we're gabbing."

"Golem," Devon said, "please ease up on Colin's partner ... a tad."

Colin glanced over at Nichts when he heard the other man raggedly gulping in some air. He had stopped struggling in the lift bot's arms, seeing that it had no effect. Colin again took note of the fluids from burst, poorly-preserved organs running down the machine's pants legs, but now he understood why they stank so.

Devon said, "To defeat the Old Ones ... well, what am I saying? You can't ever really *defeat* them. Even the Elders couldn't do that. The best they could manage was to imprison them, or put them into a kind of suspended animation. You can only thwart them ... bar them. But to do *that*, you have to use spells. Certain potent symbols and geometric drawings, certain incantations and rituals. I know you don't believe in any of that. It was hard enough to convince Missra."

"I don't."

"Ascending spells summon them to our plane, while descending spells banish them ... but I'm making it all sound far, far too easy. As you say, you wouldn't believe me anyway. But to summon an Old One without being sure you could banish it … I could never dare take such a risk."

"Why would you even want to summon one of those things in the first place?"

"To understand it … learn from it. How can you protect yourself from something you don't comprehend? And beyond learning how to protect ourselves, think of the other things we might learn from such a god-like entity!"

"Such as, how to be a god yourself?"

"This was why I chose to switch my research from creating models of various Old Ones, and trying to make those as real as possible, to creating my *own* Old One instead. I understand the hubris implicit in that statement, but I was motivated by a sense of caution! If I could create an artificial being very much like the Old Ones, with the attributes of several combined, I could study *that* instead of them with a greater sense of security. Whatever I learned from my studies could then be put to use by myself and other like-minded people and groups who take the threat of the Old Ones, and those who would see them return, more seriously!"

"But you can't help yourself, can you?" Colin said. "Even as you see the corruption from your studies spread through this city. You just want to see how much more real you can make your pet … like you did with Missra. You keep pushing it further and further. Because if you can actually create a god, then that makes you the *bigger* god, doesn't it?"

"I told you my motivations."

"Your motivation is that you've gone mad."

"I suppose I can't convince you otherwise, Colin. But now we have ourselves a problem. I have a very nice setup here and my research shows more and more promise, but here you are … come to invade my privacy and disrupt things. You leave me in a terrible spot. Yourself, as well."

"Maybe I should let Missra talk to you, after all," Colin said, though he was reluctant to lower the gun he held out in front of him in two hands so as to call Missra back on his wrist comp. "If you won't listen to me, maybe I'll give you one last chance to listen to her."

"One last chance before *what?*" Devon demanded from the speaker, his tone losing some of its former affected composure.

The robot spoke up again. "Let. Me. Eliminate. Them. Devon." Once again its powerful gloved hand tightened on Nichts' throat, causing him to gag. "They. Must. Not. Defy. Yogthutu."

"Did you hear your friend, Devon?" Colin shouted. "You think he's only trying to help you create some kind of virtual test subject? You said it yourself—his brain was infected by your system! He *worships* that thing! He wants to make it as real as any of the other Old Ones! *That's* why he's been helping you!"

"No ... " Devon said.

Just as Colin thought he should risk a shot at the robot's head, since it seemed bent on killing Nichts anyway, he saw the clone rip his own handgun out from under his coat. Nichts jammed the pistol's muzzle up under the automaton's jaw, and fired. Squeezed off three shots in total, in rapid succession, and during the mere seconds it took him to do this Colin found himself hoping Nichts didn't end up doing more harm to himself with a ricochet.

He also feared the robot would respond either purposely or reflexively by crushing Nichts in its arms, but instead—in what looked like an act of authentic rage—it tore Nichts away from its chest and flung him through the air. Nichts hit the ground hard a few feet to Colin's left, with an alarming thump, but Colin didn't look that way. Now he had his clear shot.

"Golem!" Devon called over the speaker. "No!"

For the first time he plainly saw what Devon had referred to. The front of the robot's body, exposed by the shredding of its trench coat by the shotgun's exploded crystal pellets, showed that the machine with its corrupted organic brain had pressed human organs and even balled-up wads of flesh into any nook or cranny in its only superficially anthropomorphic body of metal and ceramic. Where the shattered crystal shot had struck these organs the robot had stolen from a dead man, they had been blasted open to spray chunks of meat and stream the ichor of decomposition.

The lift bot took a step straight at Colin, which seemed to vibrate the hangar's floor it was so heavy, while reaching out its massive hands.

Colin fired twice. One gel capsule straight into the robot's torso, and then with a flick of realignment a second capsule right in the stretched mask of human flesh.

Instantly, as the two capsules burst they released their green-glowing, fast-spreading plasma. The first thing it ate away, like fire quickly consuming paper, was that unblinking mask and the human tissue wedged into its torso. The plasma then moved on to the trench coat and wide-brimmed fedora, which fell away in dripping luminous globules. Now revealed, the robot's head was mostly a blank of metal, with only a visor-like strip to see with and a thin grille to speak through.

As the flesh and garments burned away, the thing kept thumping toward Colin, even as the plasma continued to try stubbornly to seep through its thick metal plating to find more vulnerable surfaces on which to feast. But even green plasma wouldn't spread and burn forever, and already the brightness of its glow was beginning to fade.

"Don't hurt him!" Devon wailed, and Colin knew he was appealing to him not to harm the robot … not the other way around.

As if purely to spite Devon, Colin fired three more times—all at the robot's chest. He was counting on the plasma to finally work its way through those nooks and crannies where it had stuffed itself with human tissues so as to somehow, itself, feel more human. Then, he whirled toward Nichts, who was moaning and struggling to rise from where he'd been thrown. His head had struck the floor hard and he seemed to be fighting to hold on to consciousness.

Without letting go of the Revenant, Colin stopped and put one arm around Nichts, hoisted him to his feet. "Can you make it to those offices?" he asked, motioning with his head.

Nichts had managed to keep a grip on his own handgun, which was loaded with solid projectiles. "Let's get him," he wheezed.

The robot Devon called Golem kept rumbling toward them, its broad torso and metal pail of a head now hidden under a blanket of pulsating green, as if the machine were being attacked by some gigantic single-cell organism.

"You. May. Kill. Me," the lift bot said in a crackling voice now overlaid with static. "But. You. Will. Not. Kill. My. Master. Yogthutu."

Then, the robot's voice was replaced with what sounded like a recording, in a voice more fluent than the machine's own halting voice and in the words of a language Colin didn't recognize. Colin realized that the recording was in Devon's own voice.

"No, Golem, don't!" Devon pleaded helplessly from the speaker. "Not the ascending chant! Please—stop! I order you! *Don't!*"

Even with Nichts stumbling along drunkenly, supported by Colin, they outpaced the pursuing robot and were already halfway to the darkened offices at the rear of the hangar. Colin looked over his shoulder to see that the lift bot had finally stopped in its tracks, and though the plasma was fading again he felt this time it had found its way to the robot's interior. It stood there smoking from a number of joints and gaps, and yet even now it continued uttering that recording. What Devon had called an ascending chant.

"You just remember," Devon said over the speaker, and it sounded like he was actually sobbing in the process, "you did this, not me! You can blame me again all you want—but this is on you!"

The recording stuttered, faltered, and was abruptly cut off. The smoke billowing forth from the robot was heavier now, turning black, as it stood there as dead as any statue.

And yet it was too late, for Yogthutu had been summoned.

Twenty-four
Yogthutu

Just as Missra could manifest in an eyeblink, one moment the hangar was empty enough to accommodate a midsized spacecraft ... and the next it was filled with the colossal form of a god-like entity that was untold millions of years old, but at the same time had never truly existed.

Colin and Nichts backed off fast from the hunched bulk that was suddenly there beside them, flattening themselves against the hangar's metal wall and staring up at it in awe as it raised what it possessed for a head: a restless mass like the branches of a willow tree blowing madly in winds from multiple directions. This mass consisted of teeming, boneless feelers that stretched and retracted, searching the air as if to reorient the vast being to its surroundings, now that it was here again on the material plane.

When Colin had seen this being once before, reproduced in numerous holograms, it had appeared softly luminous and not entirely tangible. At least, not *this* tangible. Now, it looked to be just as much a physical object as anything else within the hangar—himself included.

The rest of the creature's body and limbs were otherwise covered in what at first might appear to be a shaggy coat of fur, but each silvery strand of it was a much shorter version of the head tentacles. Colin realized he had seen these strands before: on monitors in what he'd assumed to be the main control room of that decommissioned pollution sucker the Tikkihotto cult had dwelt in. He'd thought then that these independently moving strands resembled the thin leaves of sea plants, but now he understood they had been a close-up view of a mere portion of Yogthutu, before the entity had been fully formed to Devon's liking.

When it had first materialized, Yogthutu seemed to be crouching low to the floor in an almost frog-like position. But after it had raised the squirming chaos of its head, its body continued to straighten up ... and up. At the same time, its front limbs unfolded from where they had been tucked close to its front. Though there remained a strangely amorphous quality to the entity, despite its solidness—no line of its body sharply defined except for the fluid cord of each individual tendril—these forelimbs appeared to have more joints in them than the arms of a human being. Colin couldn't work out how many fingers it had on its hands, or whether they were jointed, too, or also tentacular.

And still the colossus straightened up its body, until it came into contact with the crisscrossing struts overhead. One might expect those rubbery-looking tendrils would give way to the seemingly firmer metal joists, but Colin heard the latter begin to squeal as they were bent ... and then torn.

"Keep moving!" he yelled to Nichts over the screeching of metal. "Hurry!"

As Colin peeled himself away from the hangar wall and helped Nichts along again toward the rear offices, he glanced back at the hardlight hologram and saw that it had fully unfolded its weirdly-jointed forelimbs, extending them upwards to push at the arched ceiling. Now, it was the hangar's roof itself that they heard tearing, as sections of the broken joists came free to drop and ring loudly across the floor around the entity's lower limbs. The dead, smoking wreck of Golem was toppled onto its side as one of the column-like silvery limbs shifted and nudged against it.

Colin hoped that in ripping its way through the ceiling, so as to further expand and achieve its full height, the creature would inadvertently cause its manifestation to end—by damaging the hangar's arrangement of holo-emitters. Unfortunately, however, the globes' position below the point where the ceiling arched had thus far prevented them from being disrupted. They might still avoid damage, even if Yogthutu continued to burst through the roof completely as the thing seemed intent on doing.

"Wait," Colin told Nichts. They paused, only steps from the rear offices. This close to their windows, he realized that rather than being painted over or the offices being kept in darkness, the glass was of the type that could be adjusted from crystal clear to black opaqueness at the touch of a button. He said, "Try shooting out some of those emitters!"

Clinging to Colin's shoulder with one arm to steady himself, Nichts raised his gun in his other hand and sighted down its length with the precision of a living machine designed to do just that. His pistol let out a crisp snap as he fired, and Colin saw with something like exaltation the green orb Nichts had aimed at explode into crystalline chunks.

"More!" Colin urged him, as the opening Yogthutu was making in the ceiling grew larger under the pressure from its forelimbs.

Nichts jerked his weapon toward another of the holo-emitters. Again, fired. Then he repeated the process with the next orb in the chain that encompassed the room. Another glittering explosion … and yet the holographic monstrosity didn't fade or flicker, or appear to grow any less solid. Its head had been thrust entirely through the hangar's roof, followed by what one might call its shoulders.

Over the speaker came Devon's voice, again chanting in that language Colin couldn't identify. At first he thought it was a recording again, but then he heard Devon gasping with sobs in the midst of the recited words. But, was he continuing the "ascending chant" Golem had used to conjure the entity, or using the "descending chant" in an effort to banish it?

If so, it appeared to be too little too late, just like the destruction of the holo-emitters.

"It isn't working!" Nichts cried. "How can that be? Is it drawing on other emitters in the area, like from the spaceport?"

"It has a life of its own now," Colin said.

With his arm around the clone's shoulders, Colin wheeled them toward the offices again … and in only a few steps they had reached the door. Colin was prepared to do anything he had to in order to open it, from using his skeleton card to melting through it with plasma, but when he stabbed the keypad the panel slid back easily to reveal a series of glass-walled, industrial-looking offices that were brightly lit rather than cloaked in darkness. He hauled Nichts through the entrance, pushed him into a nearby chair. Then, he turned to confront what lay before him.

Through the windows of the half-dozen offices, the glass of which Colin assumed could be darkened for privacy too if need be, he saw that every cubicle-like space except for the one directly in front of him was packed so full of electronics that the desks were heaped with it, leaving no room in which to move about, with the desks removed altogether in several of them. In the office to the left of the one straight ahead of him, two identical units dominated the entire space, one stacked on top of the other. Through a glass panel in the front of both units Colin saw the grayish, convoluted grooves of bioengineered tissue: the "brainframes," as they were called, of encephalon computers. These then were the two Gibster 800, cryo-cooled units stolen by Golem from Daedalus Data.

Colin stepped forward and over the threshold of the one cubicle in which there remained enough room for a man to be seated at a desk, in front of a row of monitor screens both physical and holographic. On one of these, streams of strange runes kept scrolling down and it oddly made Colin's skin crawl to gaze on them for but a second.

The man seated at the desk was slumped forward in his chair as if in despair. Colin hadn't seen Devon in quite a while, and in the past he'd known the man to wear his close-cropped hair dyed platinum blond. This man's hair had grown out a bit and was black, but Colin recognized Devon by his skin tone, as the man's father was Black and mother White. Colin had always thought of Devon as being more beautiful than handsome, and he'd resented him for that … because he'd known that it was Missra who might have described the man that way.

"Devon!" he snapped, as if to awaken a dreamer.

The chanting over the speaker abruptly ceased, but the slumped figure didn't answer, so Colin stepped closer, grabbed him by the shoulder, and spun him around in his chair. But as soon as he had put his hand on that scarecrow-like shoulder, and caught a whiff of decay, he'd known what he was going to see.

In swiveling around in the chair, the body flopped over to one side, held from falling by the chair's arm. Colin wasn't sure how long Devon Tellick had been dead, because he had obviously starved for some time before that had finally occurred. An IV bag hung empty and dry from a stand near the desk, and Colin assumed Golem had kept it filled for Devon—tended to Devon like a nurse—until one or the other of them had decided keeping that wasting shell alive was no longer necessary; a distraction from their work. The once beautiful face was sunken-cheeked and skeletal, the eyes gone a blindly-staring gray in their bony sockets. An ultranet port that Colin didn't recall Devon having possessed before, right in the center of his forehead like a third eye, trailed a cable plugged into one of the chittering, blinking pieces of equipment that crowded his desk behind the monitors.

In a corner of the little office, Devon's ghost seemed to step right out of the wall. This Devon looked equally solid—*more* substantial than the scarecrow corpse—and it retained that remembered beauty, right down to the neatly trimmed platinum hair. The man's lustrous, living brown eyes had streamed tears down his face, and yet he smiled at Colin in greeting.

"Do you even realize you're dead, Devon?" Colin asked.

"Of course, Colin. Of course. I can't say I know for how long, though. I've been in the ultranet more than out, overseeing my experiments remotely from there."

"I'm going to end this."

"I thought … " Devon looked past Colin, out toward the hangar and the crash and shriek of shredding metal. There were gunshots, too, and screaming voices as those who dwelt in Phosnoor Shipyard became aware of what was in their midst. "I truly thought that I could control it. But Golem … "

"Don't be blaming that machine," Colin said. "If you can't end this, tell me what to do. It's the Gibsters, isn't it?"

Devon smiled sadly again, and nodded. "Yes. They're the heart of it."

"If I destroy this equipment you'll be gone, won't you? Even from the ultranet."

"I will, Colin."

"Will that affect Missra's situation?"

"No. The units at my old place and Tam's will keep her alive." Devon chuckled bitterly, and he repeated in a whisper, "*Alive.*" The dead man's hardlight hologram took an imploring step toward Colin. "I ask you one favor, Colin. Can I speak to her one last time?"

"We don't have time for that!"

"It isn't fair of you to deny either of us a goodbye."

"*You* denied both of you that goodbye when you got her killed. And yourself. Don't talk fair to me now."

"You're afraid she'll try talking you out of destroying the Gibsters, because it will kill what's left of me."

"Maybe."

"She may hate you for this."

"I'll just have to live with that, then."

Colin backed out of the office, and saw Nichts was up out of his chair. The clone had peeked out of the offices into the hangar, and reported to Colin wild-eyed, "It's torn through the side of the building! It's stepped outside onto that old taxi strip! How can that be, Colin? Half the emitters are gone and now it's not even in their cross-projection!"

Colin had no time to look outside for himself. He brushed past Nichts into the open doorway of the next office on the left. Nichts jolted when he saw Devon appear in the doorway of his control center, and pointed his handgun at the apparition, but Devon's hologram could proceed no farther than that.

"Please, Colin, there has to be another way!" Devon said. "I've learned so much! I need to share my research with others like myself!"

"God forbid," Colin said.

He raised his Revenant and pointed it at the Gibster stacked atop its brother.

"*Colin!*" Devon cried, reaching out one arm desperately, while Nichts recoiled from the phantasmal limb in horror. He'd seen the corpse flopped over in its chair and realized the truth.

Two capsules of green plasma burst open against the glass pane that revealed the living brainframe beyond. Then two capsules struck the window of the lower Gibster. Colin backed out of the room again as a glowing, protoplasmic mass spread across the front of each Gibster rapidly. The two ravenous, ameba-like masses soon merged into one and the twin computers became all but obscured under these incandescent green mantles.

Waiting for the burning plasma to find its way inside the pair of powerful computers, Colin looked over again at Devon, who still stood in his doorway with one arm helplessly reaching. Slowly, he lowered it, and Colin saw fresh tears filling the dead man's eyes.

"Will you at least tell Missra I said goodbye?" he croaked.

"I will."

"And tell her ... tell her I said I'm sorry."

Colin nodded.

A sharp crack, almost like a gunshot, caused Colin to look back at the room with the Gibsters. A second gunshot sounded. He knew it was the windows that covered the two brainframes giving way.

Nichts came up beside Colin to look into the room where the plasma continued to engulf the Gibsters, not yet having faded out and dissipated. The Revenant's magazine had run empty, but with those window panels shattered Colin knew that even now the plasma had reached the organic tissue within. Green plasma liked organic material best of all.

Colin glanced again at the control room, and Devon was gone from its threshold.

Gone.

"I should have got my hands on a couple grenades before we came," Nichts said. "To blast this whole lab to pieces. That ship across the way, too."

"If the ship blew, with its engines active like that, it might kill everyone in this shipyard," Colin said. "This will be enough. It's done."

Already the holographic monitors in the control room flickered and then vanished. Physical monitors went black or showed only static at best. No more scrolling runes. Less and less lights blinked on the faces of the equipment gathered there, and in the adjoining offices as well.

"Let's get out of here," Colin said.

The top of the hangar was all but peeled away, as if a bomb had blasted straight through the ceiling. And as Nichts had said, one side wall—the one that faced out from this, the last hangar in the row, rather than into the little alley between hangars—had been ripped open to allow the massive hardlight hologram to step outside the structure.

Nichts was steadier on his feet now and no longer in need of support as the two men passed through the door into the alley by which they had entered the hangar—with Golem's unwanted assistance. They expected to see that the new day's sunlight revealed nothing but Punktown's usual skyline, perhaps with a few alien ships coming in for a landing in the nearby spaceport, bringing fresh colonists to the great city. They were wrong. Colin realized then that he should have known something was amiss, because of the continued screaming of the shipyard's inhabitants.

Tall as a building itself, silhouetted against the pale sky but glittering silver all over, Yogthutu stood in the taxi strip between the front of the demolished hangar and the boxy hauler ship that Devon and Golem had tapped into for power. The gargantuan entity seemed to be hesitating there uncertainly, its head tentacles contracting and elongating rhythmically, almost in the attitude of someone who is listening for further instructions. Was it only his imagination, or only a fervid hope, that led Colin to feel the hologram seemed somewhat less substantial than before? More like the many holograms of Yogthutu he had seen in the street outside the burnt-out convenience store.

Yes ... yes, he believed it was as Nichts had suggested. With more and more of Devon's equipment burning out and shutting down, Yogthutu was desperately drawing on other, far less powerful emitters in the vicinity to maintain a tangible form. And the vastness of Punktown was *filled* with such holo-emitters.

Nichts wagged his head in hopeless terror. "It's really in our world now! We can't kill it ... it's too late!"

A few gang kids poked their heads out from behind derelict ships, taking some more pot shots at Yogthutu with cheap guns that fired either solid bullets or streaking red rays. Neither seemed to even catch the titan's notice. Converging on the shipyard, Colin heard the approach of sirens.

"Forcers are coming," Nichts said. He put a hand on Colin's arm. "Maybe military, too. We need to leave it to them now and get out of here, Colin. We've done all we can."

Yogthutu seemed to hear these words, seemed to recognize Nichts' voice. Its entire body shifted on its two mammoth lower limbs and turned in their direction. The tendrils at the front of the weeping willow head lengthened down at them, as if to see them better, identify them better as the men who had killed the new god's maker.

"Colin!" Nichts' hand closed on his arm and squeezed. "Run!"

And Colin would have, too, had there not then come the one-two boom of a double explosion from the rear of the hangar behind him. *The Gibsters ...*

In that instant the sky above them became empty, except for the soaring towers of Punktown, with distant helicars drifting between them like bees about a hive.

Before the sirens could arrive at Phosnoor Shipyard—and with fire flickering within the shell of the ruined hangar, and black smoke billowing up through its shredded roof—Colin and Nichts hurried away, to where Colin's hot pink Razur with its yellow trim waited for them.

Epilogue
Life Changes

The mysterious virus that had spread through Punktown had subsided, leaving government experts to offer vague explanations that the citizens suspected even they didn't believe. In the absence of more satisfactory reporting, people voiced their own theories and accused authorities of a cover-up—about the bizarre events at Phosnoor Shipyard, as well.

Those who had been more severely afflicted by the mutations caused by the virus quickly died off, while those in whom the virus had not taken hold as deeply either recovered fully or were left with relatively minor damage, all things considered. For Colin, the strange headaches and concerning cramping and numbness in his right hand had abated altogether.

When Colin went to see Jolly Bill at the blue warehouse, right away he noted that the unlicensed field hospital erected there by Verge's people was gone.

Inviting Colin to sit at the two breakroom tables pushed together out on the warehouse floor, Jolly Bill was munching fried dilkies with a cup of hot mustard drink resting in front of him, which made Colin wonder for the first time if behind his profound deformities Bill was actually a Choom rather than of Earth ancestry. Colin declined refreshments and motioned with his head toward the area where the field hospital had stood.

"What about Verge?"

"He's alive, my friend, don't worry," Bill said while chewing. "But he's still so frail that his people thought it best to bring him back to their own planet. We may not see him here again, sorry to say. What a terrible loss for us."

"Mm," Colin grunted, surreptitiously glancing over at Kad Paroon, who stood a short distance away watching them. Upon entering the warehouse Colin had casually noted the position of everyone else there ... at least those he could see. Others could be hiding in the shadows, or even on top of one of the old racks with a sniper rifle, but such might be the case whenever any of Jolly Bill's most dangerous operatives paid him a visit.

"Is that all you came to talk to me about?" Bill asked. "Kad seemed to think you had something else on your mind when you called."

"Well," Colin said in a low-key tone, "I was thinking it's time for me to move on, Bill."

A silent moment elapsed. Jolly Bill stopped masticating his food. Finally the syndy boss leaned back in his chair a little, as if to appraise Colin, and said, "Oh? As in move on to another group? Like, say, the Teeb Family?"

"No, Bill. I mean, find a new line of work."

"*What?* Why would that be, my friend? Wait ... did that business with that dirty forcer Hounds shake you up?"

"Maybe it's that, a bit."

"Hey, look, you know sometimes we have to do things like that ... to send a message. To remind people we aren't to be messed with, even if those people are forcers."

"I'm not questioning that, Bill. But, I don't know what to say ... I just feel it's time."

"You really should think about this. This is a big move. I think you're being brash."

"I have thought about it."

Jolly Bill glanced toward Kad in frustration, wagging his tattooed and branded horse skull of a head. "Jesus, Colin," he sighed, "I just told you we lost Verge, and now we're going to lose you, too? Is this the way you repay me for our years of partnership?"

"We both benefitted from that relationship, and I'm grateful ... and I'm sorry ... but my mind is made up. I know I don't have any open debts with you. I'm not in possession of any materials that belong to you. So today I'd like to just shake hands and be on my way."

Bill looked back at Colin, still wagging his head as if once it was set into motion it took a while to stop, heavy as it was. "What terrible news you bring me, my friend." He threw up his hands. "But what can I say? You're not my slave, are you? You're your own man."

"Thanks for understanding."

"Well, I didn't say I understand ... I don't understand you at all ... but maybe I never really did. All I'm saying is, of course you're free to go. I just wish you wouldn't."

Colin stood up from the table and extended his hand. "Thanks, Bill."

Jolly Bill took the offered hand and squeezed it. "Are you leaving Punktown, then, is that it?"

"I don't think so."

Once more, Bill sat back in his chair and seemed to be trying to see right into Colin. At last he said, "Then maybe we'll run into each other again someday."

Colin wasn't sure if that statement implied something more beneath the surface, but he only smiled mildly and said, "See ya." Then he turned away, and Kad Paroon fell in beside him to walk him out of the blue warehouse.

"If you got any more money coming your way, Colin," the Choom said, "I'll find out and be sure you get it."

"I believe the slate's clean, Kad."

When they reached the side door that opened into the gated parking lot, Kad paused and said, "You know, Colin, Bill gets nervous when people who know a lot about his business and the people in it decide to leave the ranks."

Colin gave a little shrug. "It's good to stay a bit on the nervous side, Kad. Keeps you on your toes. I mean, I may not look it, but I'm *always* on my toes."

With Kad's veiled threat dealt, along with Colin's counterthreat, the two men shook hands and Colin walked toward his Razur. He kept his eyes away from another hovercar parked across the street and a little further down, in which Nichts had been sitting with his wrist comp open, just like Colin's, listening in case Colin needed backup. An AE-93 Sturm assault engine lay across the Blue War veteran's thighs.

However, the gate in the parking lot's fence was drawn aside and Colin's Razur was allowed to pass through without any resistance on the part of Jolly Bill's crew, and so Nichts started his own vehicle into motion and followed Colin away.

Colin had, in fact, briefly entertained the idea of introducing the Blue War clone to Jolly Bill and recommending him as a replacement for Verge until the tiny being recovered—this, before Colin had learned Verge had left Oasis for his home world. Maybe Nichts wasn't quite the tech wiz Verge was, but he had the advantage of being a seasoned soldier. With the rest of the team at Ronin Security dead, Nichts would be needing new employment. He was a fierce pack animal without a pack.

Then, Colin had come upon another idea, and now that he had formally severed his bond with the syndy he pointed the Razur toward his new place of employment.

When he'd hit upon the idea, before proposing it to Nichts he'd first asked the clone, "The work your crew did at Ronin Security … was it actually mercenary stuff, or real security work?"

"Whatever gigs we could get," Nichts had explained. "From the legit to the less than legit."

Well, that meant their outfit was about as clean as one might realistically expect for Punktown. Colin had then gone on to share with Nichts his proposal … and here they were now, arriving at the office of Ronin Security as two members of its new team.

As it turned out, the Ronin office was in Subtown, only half a dozen blocks from Colin's apartment building. Nichts let the two of them in, then turned to Colin and grinned. "This is cause for celebration, isn't it?"

"I think we could indulge."

While Nichts passed into another room, in which could be heard the clinking of bottles as the veteran looked for just the right one, the third member of the new Ronin Security team appeared before Colin.

"Did you do it?" Missra asked him.

"I did it," he said.

The day before, he and Nichts had removed whatever equipment they needed from Devon's apartment, including the holo-emitters. There wouldn't be a need to go back there again, and their respective landlords could do whatever they liked with the rest of the sad belongings Devon Tellick and Tam Vonner had left behind, like the words of unread obituaries. Now those holo-emitters were installed in these rooms, giving Missra the freedom to pass between Ronin Security—her new place of employment—and Colin's apartment at will.

"I'm happy for you, Colin," Missra said, stepping aside a bit as Nichts remerged bearing two glasses of whiskey, sans ice, and handing one to Colin.

"No drinking for you," Nichts joked to Missra.

"No wonder. I'm only a few months old," she replied.

"Oh hey, stop with that talk," Nichts chided her. He raised his glass to Colin. "To the new Ronin Security."

"Keeping Punktown safe from interdimensional entities since two days ago," Missra said, miming the raising of a third glass.

When Colin and Nichts had returned to his apartment from Phosnoor Shipyard, and told Missra what had occurred there—and about the fate of Devon Tellick—Colin had been prepared for anger, recriminations. Why hadn't he allowed her to speak to Devon one last time and plead with him? Instead, to Colin's relief she had only lowered her head and begun to weep. Just as with Devon's hologram, Colin saw convincing tears running down her cheeks.

"I'm sorry," he told her. "And Devon asked me to tell you that he was sorry, too."

Missra nodded, gasped back a sob, and said, "I want to believe that the reason he kept going, making Yogthutu stronger and more real, was because that robot was influencing him. Or maybe being hooked up like that to his system, a corruption got into his brain, too, just like it did with Golem. I want to believe the old Devon, the man I knew—who only wanted to protect people—would never have allowed things to get that out of control."

Colin had hesitated, then stepped toward her and reached out a hand to place on Missra's arm. And he actually felt something there ... not exactly substantial, but not empty air either. When he did this, Missra lifted her head and met his eyes. Something unspoken but understood passed between them.

And today, here they were ... and Colin and Nichts gulped back their whiskey in one swallow.

"Another?" Nichts said, grinning again hopefully.

"Not on the job," Colin said. "We've got work to do. We need to make sure we weed out any of your old gear that might have been compromised by that virus you picked up from Tam ... just to be sure."

"About that," Missra said. "There's something I wanted to tell you guys."

Colin and Nichts looked toward her expectantly. They saw that her expression had turned grim.

"Maybe it's nothing," she said. "I hope it's nothing. It isn't on the news, but on the net I saw a few people here in Punktown claiming they'd witnessed some strange things."

"Strange things?" Colin asked.

"In a discussion of what happened at Phosnoor Shipyard, these people claimed they'd seen holographic signs for restaurants and businesses, or whatever, change for just a second or two. What they saw matches the descriptions from people who were at the shipyard and saw Yogthutu for themselves."

"Witnesses made vids of that thing with their wrist comps," Nichts countered, "and shared them on the net. It would be easy for these people to lie, just as a prank or to get some attention."

"Was this at the same time Yogthutu appeared at the shipyard?" Colin asked. "Maybe at the same time it was trying to draw on other emitters in the area?"

"No. These reports all came from yesterday. The day *after* you two went there."

Colin went to a window of the main office room, and stood there gazing out at this subterranean neighborhood of the megacity that its inhabitants called Punktown.

"It's still out there. Waiting in the ultranet … or somewhere else." He set down his empty whiskey glass, because there truly was work to do. "It's real now. And it wants to come back."

About the Author

JEFFREY THOMAS is the author of the dark science fiction series Punktown, which was introduced with the collection *Punktown* (Ministry of Whimsy Press, 2000) and includes the novels *Monstrocity* (Prime Books, 2003; Bram Stoker Award finalist), *Deadstock* (Solaris Books, 2007; John W. Campbell Award finalist), and *Blue War* (Solaris Books, 2008). His other books include the short story collection *The Unnamed Country* (Word Horde, 2019), the novel *The American* (JournalStone, 2020), and the Hades Trilogy (Weird House Press, 2023). His stories have been reprinted in *The Year's Best Horror Stories XXII* (editor, Karl Edward Wagner), *The Year's Best Fantasy and Horror #14* (editors, Ellen Datlow and Terri Windling), and *Year's Best Weird Fiction #1* (editors, Laird Barron and Michael Kelly). Thomas lives in Massachusetts.

About the Artist

Born in Pennsylvania, MICHAEL SQUID is a horror author and filmmaker. His unique and chilling stories have appeared in several books, anthologies, podcasts, and comic adaptations. A film lover and horror devourer, he began bringing his dark concepts to film with his debut short, *The Chrysalis*.

www.ingramcontent.com/pod-product-compliance
Lightning Source LLC
Chambersburg PA
CBHW030324020726
47493CB00004B/1156